Cold Front

Echoes In the Frost

(A Crimson Alliance interlude)

Acknowledgement

Writing *Cold Front: Echoes in the Frost* was an entirely different journey than its predecessor *A Demon's Rebellion: The Rise of Lilith* – quieter in some ways, yet no less fierce in its emotional depth and humor. This book would not exist without the foundations laid in its predecessor, nor without the friends, mentors, and readers who continue to champion the world of the Crimson Alliance Universe.

To those who encouraged me to explore the quiet strength of Kimiko, the fierce loyalty of Freija, and the complex stillness of Frigid, I humbly thank you. You reminded me that growth often begins in the silence between battles.

To the readers who asked for more Icelandia, more myth, more mystery then this story is for you. Thank you for seeing the potential in the spaces left unexplored.

To my beta readers and early supporters, who provided clarity, laughter, and the occasional reality check, you helped shape this book into something worth returning to, time and again.

And finally, to the elemental forces of inspiration, late-night sessions, and stubborn determination, may the next journey be just as haunting, just as beautiful.

~ K. A. Dunlap

Cold Front

Echoes In the Frost

(A Crimson Alliance interlude)

K.A. Dunlap

Cold Front: Echoes In the Frost
© 2025 by K.A. Dunlap

All rights reserved.

ISBN:
Hardcover: 979-8-9929819-3-3
Paperback: 979-8-9929819-2-6

Contact the Author

K.A. Dunlap

KADunlap@TheCAU.net

Website: https://www.TheCAU.net

Cover design by:
Interior formatting by:
Published by:

First Edition

Table of Contents

Character Preface: The Story So Far

A Crimson Alliance Interlude (featuring Freija, Kimiko, and Frigid) – Part of: The Crimson Alliance saga

Kimiko

Kimiko, recently turning 29, was born of royal blood in Kyoto, Japan, the daughter of a renowned warrior who walked the edge of both tradition and secrecy. From her earliest years, she was raised in the silent discipline of the samurai and ninja – trained to move without sound, strike without hesitation, and endure without complaint. She became the perfect weapon in a world that had no use for names, only results. Her life was ruled by order... by codes... by purpose.

But fate reshaped her path. A galactic war called her from the shadows, offering not a target, but a choice. She joined Lilith and the Crimson Alliance – seven warriors united across the stars to confront a rising darkness. Kimiko did not seek heroism. She sought purpose, and in the fires of battle, she found comradeship and cause.

She fights with twin katanas strapped across her back and a pair of black steel sai at her hips. Though trained in firearms, she relies on blade and silence, not gunfire, to cut through the chaos of war.

Freija

Freija, the younger of two royal identical twins by ten minutes, was born 112 years ago (on her world she was still considered early-mid maturity) into ice and light on a world called Icelandia. Only five-foot-two, with short white hair, cobalt-blue wings, blue skin, and eyes that sparkled like frozen stars, she embraced her role not with formality, but with laughter. Lighthearted and free-spirited, Freija found joy in flight, mischief, and defying rules, especially those meant to keep her grounded.

Though she was born a princess, her spirit soared far beyond the royal halls. She answered Lilith's call and became one of seven warriors in the Crimson Alliance, each chosen for their strength and soul. In the chaos of war, Freija proved herself not only as a fighter, but as a beacon of hope. She chose to stand beside Kimiko not only on the battlefield but as a devoted friend.

Freija wields twin ice-born short swords, forged from enchanted glacier metal. Each blade can release precision bursts of magical ice shards – projectiles as deadly as her close-combat strikes. Around her neck hangs the Frostheart charm given by her twin, a reminder of home during battles fought on faraway stars.

Frigid

Frigid was born first as the elder twin... however, that small margin came the weight of her destiny. Standing the same height as Freija, with the same cobalt-white wings but long flowing white hair and blue skin, Frigid was destined to rule as Queen of Icelandia. Her life had been shaped by centuries-old rituals and expectations, carved from ice and duty. She was meticulous, graceful, and unwavering, every gesture a reflection of the crown she was born to wear.

She remained behind when the stars called her sister away, not from fear, but from devotion. Her world was one of structure and solemn responsibility, and she upheld it with pride. Yet even within her composed exterior stirred a quiet yearning... a flicker of doubt that wondered what lay beyond the frost-covered gates. Her loyalty to her people was absolute. But her heart, slowly, had begun to ask if loyalty alone made a ruler whole.

Frigid carries a ceremonial double-bladed spear, sleek, balanced, and reinforced with elemental sigils of her lineage. Each end is honed to perfection, allowing for elegant sweeps, twin strikes, and full-circle defense. Her elemental mastery over ice surpasses even Freija's, though she invokes it sparingly... and only when absolutely necessary.

Prelude: The Codex of Icelandia

Before the stars beckoned. Before frostcraft gave way to science. Before wings pierced the skies beyond the clouds – there was only Icelandia.

A small Mars-sized world cloaked in snow and myth, Icelandia was born of elemental fury and sculpted by wind, ice, and time. It turned slowly around a red dwarf sun, its skies veiled in eternal twilight. Though the planet brimmed with glacial beauty, its history was far from serene. For much of its early millennia, Icelandia was divided – a fractured world of cold ambition and ancient rivalries.

There are four great continents on Icelandia:

- The **Northern Continent**, called **Icecrest** crowned by the royal city of Frostholm, where the icy mountains split the heavens and the sky sings with auroras.
- The **Southern Continent**, called **Dorland**, a land of frost plains and rich mineral veins, known for trade and stubborn independence.
- The **Eastern Continent**, called **Skarae**, a jagged land of volcanic ridges and geothermal vents, where the sky is often painted in ash and steam.
- The **Western Continent**, known as **Sommara**, whose cliffs plunge into black-ice seas and whose people once spoke only in song.

Each continent was ruled by a sovereign court, each claiming divine right over their lands. Though the Icelandian people shared their avian ancestry – each born with wings, hollow bones, and frost-resistant skin – they warred endlessly. Icecrest from the North clashed with Dorland from the South over trade routes. Skarae in the East sought to harness the heat beneath the ice for power. Sommara in the West remained insular, refusing all treaties, hoarding ancient knowledge in secretive libraries of obsidian stone.

There was no unity. No alliance. Only frost-covered blades and frozen battlefields.

Until one king tried to change everything.

His name has been lost to time, though his legacy endures in the bones of the North. He was a visionary king of the Icecrest – young, fierce, and gifted in both swordplay and statecraft. Unlike his predecessors, he dreamed not of conquest but of connection. He imagined a world where the skies were not divided by borderlines and winged warriors but shared in peace and prosperity.

Trade. Harmony. Peace. A unified Icelandia.

The other kings laughed at his proposals. The king of Dorland dismissed him as naive. The king of Skarae called him a dreamer. Sommara refused to even respond. Frustrated by centuries of bloodshed and deadlock, the young king turned to the only power he believed could unite them all… ancient magic.

In the frozen catacombs beneath Frostholm, he gathered the last of the old mages – those whose knowledge predated the First Frost, whose voices still resonated with the raw elemental forces that shaped the planet. He sought their counsel, demanded their guidance.

They warned him of the cost. Magic that could sway the world was never pure. It was bound to be tethered to things buried… to entities that slumbered beneath the ice long before the winged people had ever drawn breath. But the king would not be deterred.

Together, the mages and the king performed a great summoning.

It began beneath the northern sky, beneath a rare full triad moon. They carved runes into the glaciers, bled frost and fire into sigils, and chanted words that had not been spoken in ten generations. And from the rift between realms came the creature – a spectral entity of frost and storm, born of thought and bound by command.

It had no face, no voice. Only wings of ice and a crown of shifting crystal. It bowed to the king, bound by the magic that called it forth. The king named it *Iskarion*, the Harbinger of Unity.

The other continents, sensing the North's growing power, responded with their own summoning. Skarae conjured a fire-being of molten ash. Dorland raised a golem of air and wind. Sommara, most dangerous of all, tore through their own forbidden tomes and summoned an earth-wraith clad in obsidian armor.

But none could match Iskarion.

The Harbinger moved with terrifying grace, devouring the other spectral creatures in a series of battles that shook the very skies. It grew stronger with each victory, feeding not just on magic, but on memory and fear. And as its power swelled, so too did its ambition.

Iskarion turned on the northern king.

"I will unify this world," it declared in a voice that froze rivers. "But not for you. For myself."

The betrayal came swiftly. Cities in Icecrest were consumed by eternal ice storms. The air shimmered with auric frost. The Harbinger carved its own throne into the heart of a mountain – Mount Solance – and began to call forth other shadows from beneath the world.

Realizing the horror they had unleashed, the four rulers – once enemies – joined together. The mages, too, cast aside their rivalries and united under a single spell-circle, etched deep into the bones of Icelandia. With their combined strength, they cast the greatest banishment ever attempted.

But it was not only their magic that made it possible. One among the old elemental beings, long forgotten by the world, answered the call to restore balance. Neither born of ice nor fire, wind nor stone, it came cloaked in stillness and heart—a force older than ambition, known only in whispered texts as *the Gatekeeper*.

With its aid, the Harbinger was forced into sleep. Not slain – for such a being could not die – but sealed beneath Mount Solance, entombed in a crystalline vault of living frost. The magic was layered in millennia, drawn from every continent, every school, every cost.

The Vault became legend. A myth told to keep children from wandering too deep into the ice.

But beneath it all, Iskarion dreamt.

And Icelandia – for all its unity in the centuries that followed – still trembles in the silence beneath its peaks.

The Next Adventure

The galaxy, for a brief moment, exhaled.

After the firestorms of war, after the fall of Necra and the unraveling of her obsidian armada, the stars burned calmly once more. Systems long divided by bloodshed and silence began to pulse with life again – slowly, cautiously, but undeniably. And at the heart of that fragile peace stood seven warriors who had held the line… the Crimson Alliance.

Lilith, the demon-turned-liberator, had looked at them each in turn – bloodied, battle-worn, and still standing – and declared the impossible.

"You've earned a break."

Not just a day or a week, but three full months. Time to heal. Time to breathe. Time to rediscover who they were without war snarling at their heels.

Their next gathering would be at Nefertari's newly constructed command center on the world of Velyria, a former battleground now being transformed into a symbol of renewal and alliance. The Crimson Alliance would reconvene, reorganize, and decide what came next. But until then, Lilith had ordered rest. True rest. The kind of pause that left warriors unsettled but desperately needed.

FREIJA

Each of the team members went off into different reaches of the galaxy.

However, for Freija, the answer was clear… Icelandia, her home.

Icelandia awaited, cloaked in frost and silence. A planet untouched by the chaos of the wider galaxy, and yet no less complex beneath its glacial surface. It was where her wings first stretched in childhood flight, where the burden of royalty first pressed down on her shoulders. But it was also where memories had frozen in place, and where she hoped the cold might offer something the battlefield never could… clarity.

Kimiko hadn't asked to join her.

She didn't need to.

KIMIKO

In the quiet days following the final battle, while debris still drifted in orbit and the smell of scorched metal lingered in corridors, Freija approached her in the hangar of the Scorpion. Kimiko had been cleaning her twin katanas, the blade edges gleaming in artificial light, her face expressionless.

"You don't have to go back to Earth," Freija had said, softly. "Come with me. Icelandia's not warm – but it's honest. And I think you could use some honest rest."

Kimiko paused, considered, and nodded. Not because she needed somewhere to go. But because for the first time in a long while, someone had offered a gift without expecting anything in return.

A Transport to Icelandia

Days into their journey aboard a mid-sized civilian transport retrofitted for long-distance travel, the silence between them was companionable. The ship – old, functional, and mostly reliable – was configured for basic comfort. It was unremarkable by design, drifting through quiet lanes of space without attracting notice. But, it was enough.

Freija would spend long hours at the forward viewport, wrapped in a thermal shawl the color of periwinkle ice, legs tucked beneath her, wings occasionally fluttering. Sometimes she hummed softly, tunes from her childhood – melodies the palace staff used to sing when the sun barely rose above the glaciers. Songs with no lyrics, only feeling.

Often, her fingers would find their way to the Frostheart pendant hanging around her neck. A gift from her twin sister, Frigid – given in the quiet of a dim hallway before Freija had left Icelandia. The gem pulsed faintly with a gentle blue glow, casting flickers of light against her blue skin. She would run her thumb over it absentmindedly, remembering her sister's cool hands fastening it in place, and the unspoken worry that had lingered in her eyes.

Kimiko kept to the training hold. Her katanas moved in deliberate arcs, dancing like silver flames in her hands. She cycled through katas and routines without pause, her body a study in focus. There was no enemy now, but the discipline remained. It was how she stayed grounded. Her movements echoed quietly through the metallic corridors, rhythmic, meditative.

Occasionally, Freija would drift into the training hold and watch from the doorway, arms crossed, expression unreadable. Kimiko never acknowledged her presence, but she never asked her to leave either. Their bond was wordless in those moments – built not on shared sentiment, but on mutual respect forged in the fire of battle.

They didn't need words.

Not yet.

But the journey wasn't just through space – it was through healing. And both were learning how to exist without danger defining them.

Ahead lay Icelandia… a world blanketed in silence, veined with glowing crystal formations and towering ice spires. Its skies shimmered with auroras most evenings, and its winds whistled through the mountain passes and valleys, channeling echoes of ancient songs along the sculpted ice and stone.

Kimiko had never seen it.

Freija had never shared it.

Now, together, they approached something far more unfamiliar than war.

Peace.

And beneath that stillness, something ancient waited – not with menace, but with memory.

Echoes in the Ice

The cold hit differently this time.

As the transport ship descended through the cloud-draped skies of Icelandia, Freija stared out of the narrow viewport, her breath misting against the frosted glass. Jagged mountain ridges stretched below, draped in endless sheets of ice and snow. Frostholm shimmered in the distance, still as regal as she remembered – but dimmer somehow. Weaker. The wind howled like a voice she almost recognized, and the air felt tighter, as though the planet itself were holding its breath.

Beside her, Kimiko stood next to her in silence. Her dark eyes scanned the landscape, her hands resting calmly at her sides. Freija could sense the tension beneath her stoic demeaner. The ninja's stillness was never idle – it was always the quiet before movement, the pause before the strike.

Freija exhaled softly and smiled. "Looks inviting, doesn't it?"

Kimiko didn't blink. "No."

Freija laughed under her breath. "Fair."

Kimiko tilted her head slightly, the shadow of a smirk threatening the corners of her lips. "How cold are we talking?"

Freija stretched, letting her wings unfurl a bit outside of her cloak. "Colder than your darkest training pit. The kind of cold that freezes your breath before it leaves your mouth. It sinks into your bones and starts whispering secrets."

"Sounds like home," Kimiko said dryly.

Their banter faded as the landing sequence initiated. The ship rocked gently under their feet as landing gear extended. Blue indicator lights flared to life across the control panels. Freija watched the palace draw nearer – those towering icy spires cutting into the sky like crystal knives.

The transport touched down on the landing pad with a gentle thud. Snow swept across the reinforced glass, dancing in little vortices as the ramp lowered with a hiss. Freija stepped out into the cold first, her boots crunching into the snow-packed landing platform. The air hit her like a spell – sharp and biting, pure in a way no other world ever managed to her.

The Frostheart charm at her neck pulsed with cool light, reacting to the proximity of home. She reached up and touched it briefly, feeling a weight of emotion coil in her chest. She hadn't seen her sister in over six months. Frigid's last message had been clipped, cautious, and masked in a political tone.

But she could sense that there was fear in it. The kind that wasn't spoken aloud.

Two rows of guards in polished ice-forged armor stood at attention on either side of the walkway, their faces hidden beneath visors that shimmered with protective enchantments. Their wings stretched in a royal defensive position. No fanfare. No formal greeting. Just eyes – watching. Waiting. Silent.

At the end of the line, standing alone before the palace gates, was Frigid.

FRIGID

Her long white hair rippled in the wind, woven through with delicate strands of glacial silk. Her robes were ceremonial, but subtly armored, and a polished sigil of Parliament glinted at her shoulder. Her blue face was pale with exhaustion, but her back remained straight, her presence unshaken. When she saw Freija, her cool expression faltered for only a moment – just enough to let something real surface.

"Sister," she said.

"Frigid!" replied Freija in excitement.

They met halfway, and Freija threw her arms around her without hesitation. The hug was fierce yet fleeting – like something they'd both

15

needed but didn't want to linger on too long. When they pulled apart, Frigid's gaze slid to Kimiko.

"You've brought company."

Freija smiled. "This is Kimiko. Crimson Alliance teammate. Deadlier than she looks."

Kimiko bowed slightly in the traditional Icelandian way, "Princess."

Frigid returned the gesture with a subtle nod. "Welcome to Icelandia."

They turned toward the palace, boots crunching over fresh snow. The guards remained in place, their movements precise, their stillness unnerving. There was something in the air – a tension that hadn't existed before.

"What happened here?" Freija asked quietly.

Frigid's lips were tight. "A lot. Too much. And not enough that anyone's willing to name."

Inside the palace, warmth from a fire burning in various hearths took the edge off the cold. Hallways of sculpted ice gleamed beneath their boots, and echoes of their footsteps followed them all the way to the grand hall. There, King Frostran and Queen Glaciana waited – regal, poised, unreadable.

The Sigil Misstep

The three were making their way to the grand hall where Kimiko and Frigid walked side-by-side and Freija followed close behind, almost skipping as she went along. Kimiko was taking in the shifting blue light along the carved walls. Her gaze was focused upward, until she nearly stepped directly onto a glowing sigil embedded in the floor.

Frigid's hand shot out. "Stop!"

Kimiko froze mid-step, her boot hovering centimeters above the swirling glyph embedded into the floor. The energy within the sigil pulsed once, almost as if acknowledging her presence.

"I… I…" Kimiko began.

"It's ceremonial," Frigid said quickly, recovering her composure. "To step on it is... frowned upon."

Kimiko pulled her foot back and gave a slow, respectful nod. "Understood."

Freija, trailing behind, walked right across the next sigil with deliberate exaggeration. "Oh no, I've insulted our ancestors... again."

Frigid gave a long-suffering sigh and muttered, "There she goes again."

Kimiko looked over her shoulder at Frigid. "Is she always like this at home?"

"Yes," Frigid said.

"And somehow worse," Freija added with a cheerful grin.

The moment defused the tension. Even Frigid's lips twitched with the hint of a smile as they resumed their walk to the king's chambers.

Meeting the Royals

King Frostran and Queen Glaciana waited – regal and poised, though smaller in stature than Kimiko had expected. The King stood at five-foot-six, his posture straight as a blade. The Queen, equally composed, stood five-foot-four – Kimiko's exact height.

KING FROSTRAN

"Daughter," the King said, his tone controlled. "And a guest from beyond our stars."

Queen Glaciana's gaze lingered thoughtfully on Kimiko. "It is rare for our halls to host one born of another world."

Kimiko offered a respectful Icelandian bow. "Your Majesties."

The Queen's voice remained gentle, though her words carried weight. "You are far from home. Does Icelandia strike you as inhospitable?"

Kimiko answered evenly. "Unfamiliar, yet not unkind."

QUEEN GLACIANA

The King studied her for a moment, then turned to Freija. "Your friend has a curious tongue."

Freija grinned. "You should hear her when she's irritated."

Queen Glaciana's expression shifted to mild amusement. "And do you find us irritating, off-worlder?"

Kimiko responded with calm precision. "I find you gracious, Your Majesty. Though your customs take some learning."

The Queen gave a nod of acknowledgment. "That is fair."

Frostran's gaze returned to his daughter. "You've come home... changed."

"Experience tends to do that," Freija replied, her voice light but steady.

"Some experiences," Frostran said pointedly, "change more than just the person."

Kimiko remained completely silent.

Frigid's voice broke the tension. "Father. We are grateful for your welcome. We won't overstay it."

Queen Glaciana's eyes narrowed slightly. "See that you don't."

But then she offered the smallest of smiles, almost invisible. "You are still our daughters. Both of you."

Freija's expression softened, but she said nothing.

Frostran nodded curtly. "Go. Rest. We will speak later."

With that, the King and Queen turned, and the meeting ended.

Freija's Chambers

Afterward, the sisters and Kimiko retreated to Freija's old chambers – still preserved as if she had never left. There, for the first time since landing, Freija exhaled dramatically.

"That went better than I expected."

Kimiko raised an eyebrow. "That was better?"

Freija chuckled. "You've never seen my father truly annoyed."

Frigid stood by the frost-glass window, gazing out over the city. "They were cautious. But grateful. You both fought in a war that its ramifications even reached our quiet litttle planet... whether the council admits it or not."

Kimiko tilted her head slightly. "And now?"

Frigid turned, her expression unreadable. "Now... Now you are guests... And, we treat guests with honor."

Frigid led them out of Freija's chambers and through a side corridor, away from the throne room and into a private council chamber sealed with a rune-etched door. Once inside, she waved her hand over the lock. The runes dimmed, then glowed faintly blue.

"No ears here," she said. "At least... I hope not."

Freija raised an eyebrow. "Frigid, what's going on?"

Frigid didn't answer immediately. She crossed the room to a small crystal decanter, poured herself a measure of glacier wine, and drank. Then she poured another.

Finally, she turned, her voice lower. "Everything is wrong. And I don't know where to begin."

Kimiko remained silent, listening.

Frigid paced as she spoke. "It started with whispers. Not rumors –
actual whispers. In the ice. In the halls. Even in our dreams. The glaciers
are… speaking. I've heard them myself. And the weather – it's growing
more violent. Unpredictable. Villages in the north have gone silent. No
messages. No trade. No bodies were found, either. Just… silence."

Freija's stomach turned. "Why haven't you called for help?"

"I did," Frigid said softly. "But the Parliament insisted on secrecy.
They think it's internal. A local disturbance. They won't risk spreading
panic. And Father…"

She trailed off.

Freija stepped closer. "What about Father, Frigid?"

Frigid's eyes met hers. They were glassy, wet with a shimmer of
fear Freija had never seen there before. "He's not himself. He says he's
protecting us – fortifying ancient wards deep in the foundation. But the
magic he's using… I don't recognize it. It's not frostcraft. It's something
older… Hungrier."

Kimiko finally spoke. "Dark magic?"

Frigid didn't flinch. "Yes… I believe so."

The chamber grew colder.

"I don't know what he's done," Frigid continued. "But I've seen the
runes. They absorb light. The walls near his private sanctum are starting
to… shift. They hum. Like they're alive."

Freija's hands clenched. "Does Mother know?"

Frigid shook her head. "She trusts him. She thinks his strange
behavior is the weight of leadership. But I've been watching him. And
I'm telling you, Freija… he's hiding something. Something dangerous."

Silence fell between the three women, broken only by the distant
creaking of the palace ice.

Frigid walked to a shelf and retrieved a small wooden box. Inside
lay a jagged shard of obsidian ice wrapped in silk. It pulsed faintly; its
surface etched with eerie runes.

"This was found embedded in the heart of an abandoned village
temple," she said. "I don't know what it is, but it radiates the same energy
I feel near Father's chambers."

Kimiko stepped closer, studying the shard. "Is this not native to this
world?"

Frigid stared at it. "It's starting again."

Freija looked at her. "What is?"

"The war," Frigid said. "Or something like it."

Freija looked down at the Frostheart charm around her neck, its glow now brighter than before.

Kimiko moved to the window. Her voice was soft. "This planet feels like it's being watched."

Freija joined her, looking out at the swirling snow.

From behind they heard Frigid continue, "That's because it is. Something is stirring in the ice. And it doesn't want to be found. Or maybe… it does."

Frigid took a deep breath. "There's more. A hidden cavern beneath Mount Solance has been uncovered by a quake. Sealed for millennia. It wasn't on any royal map. The Parliament is pretending it doesn't exist… but I sent scouts."

She looked between them sternly. "None returned."

A silence stretched long and heavy.

"We'll go," Freija said.

Kimiko didn't hesitate. "Tomorrow morning when we have light."

Frigid looked between them. Then, in a rare moment of softness, she stepped forward and reached into a velvet-lined drawer in the corner of the room. From it, she retrieved a second Frostheart pendant – nearly identical to the one Freija wore. It shimmered in the dim light, pulsing faintly with an inner bluish glow.

She approached Kimiko and held it out.

"For luck," Frigid said. "And because you've earned more than just respect."

Kimiko accepted it without a word. She fastened the chain around her neck, letting the cool weight settle against her tunic. The gem pulsed once – warm, then still.

Freija smiled. "It looks good on you."

Kimiko's fingers brushed the pendant once before letting her hand fall. "Thank you."

No more words were needed.

The next day, they would leave for Mount Solance.

And whatever waited in the ice.

Mission Parameters

A New Mission

Snow whispered down from the dark sky in a slow, constant descent. Outside the royal palace, twilight never truly lifted on Icelandia this far north, only shifting shades from blue-gray to silver-white. A quiet storm curled around the ancient walls, rattling frost-crusted windows and weaving itself into every breath.

Kimiko moved like a shadow through the corridor's curves, her boots silent on the frost-slick floor. She studied the etched runes that lined the walls – elegant and ancient – but their glow was dimmed here, almost sickly. As she rounded a corner, she found Freija waiting near a high arched window, arms folded, wings tucked tight against her back.

The princess's gaze was fixed on the courtyard far below, where guards changed shifts with the precision of a planet that feared uncertainty. The wind pushed at the windows like it wanted inside.

"Is your world always this cold?" Kimiko asked, coming to stand beside her.

Freija smirked. "Worse in the winter. It's mid-Spring now."

Kimiko studied her for a long moment. Freija's short white hair was wind-tossed and spiky, her cobalt-blue skin even paler in the silver sunlight. The Frostheart charm glowed faintly at her throat. She had wrapped herself in silence since the conversation with Frigid, but Kimiko knew better than to push. Not yet.

"I think I liked it better when it was just rumors," Freija said finally.

"The whispers in the ice?" Kimiko asked inquisitively.

"Those… and whatever Father's hiding. Frigid's calm, but I could see it in her eyes. She's scared."

Kimiko nodded. "She's right to be."

They turned as the door behind them opened. Frigid stepped in, her cloak trailing faint frost in her wake. Her wings partially extended, indicating some excitement. She carried a rolled parchment in one hand, a sealed crystal in the other.

"This is what I could get from the Archives," she said, laying the map across the nearest table. It unfurled with a quiet crackle – parchment edged with delicate filigree and arcane markings. "This pass leads to a deep cavern system beneath Mount Solance. It wasn't on our official maps until the quake reopened it. I suspect it was sealed on purpose."

Freija and Kimiko leaned in.

"Your guide will meet you at the eastern drop point. He's loyal, though… unconventional." Frigid hesitated. "His name is Kael. You'll recognize him by the wolf crest on his armor's shoulder."

Freija nodded. "How unstable is the route?"

"Enough that we haven't sent another team since the first one vanished. And the magic near the entrance has grown erratic. Don't trust anything you see once you're inside."

Kimiko frowned. "Illusions?"

"Worse," Frigid responded

Frigid looked down at the Frostheart charm around Freija's neck. It pulsed steadily now, like a second heartbeat. The charm around Kimiko's neck was pulsating in a similar manner.

"These charms do react to danger," Freija added. "Heatless pulses. If you feel it throbbing, something's coming. And it might be a threat."

Kimiko looked down at the charm around her neck. "Understood."

Frigid touched Freija's arm. "Be careful. I mean it. I've seen ice bleed before. But not like this."

Freija softened. "We'll be back."

Frigid stepped away, her face composed, but her eyes lingered too long on her sister.

Beginning on the Path

Their glide craft waited at the outer harbor, a two-person vessel, low-winged and rune-cloaked. Freija took the pilot's seat, fingers dancing on controls that hummed in keyed pulses of blue.

"Guide us through this?" Kimiko asked as she settled beside her, kneeling to check both katanas in their sheaths. Her two sai were also at her waist, holstered like an Earth gunslinger from the old West.

Freija exhaled softly. "I'm nervous and apprehensive as to what we'll find. But… I know this is what we have to do."

The vessel plummeted down between jagged peaks. Below stretched ice ridges and plateaus, silent glaciers groaning in their own slow drift, cracks glowing faintly from deep strain.

Kimiko peered out through the side canopy, eyes narrowing. "It's hard to believe anything could live down there."

Freija gave a tight nod. "Not much does. But the old things… they don't count as 'alive' the way you're thinking."

"Comforting," Kimiko muttered.

They dipped lower, skimming the rim of a massive basin where wind had carved fluted spirals into the snow. Shards of crystalline ice jutted from the surface like the ribs of long-dead beasts.

"Icelandia doesn't do gentle terrain, does it?" Kimiko said, trying to mask her unease with humor.

Freija smirked. "We consider this scenic."

A deep chasm cut through the next ridgeline, its sheer walls layered with centuries of compacted frost. Mist billowed upward in thin, twisting columns.

"Do you trust Kael?" Kimiko asked suddenly.

"I trust Frigid. That's enough, for now."

Kimiko leaned back, letting her head rest against the seat. "I hate not knowing what we're walking into."

Freija's hands tightened on the controls. "So do I. But we're not alone." She glanced sideways, the corner of her mouth softening. "You've been through worse."

Kimiko nodded. "Doesn't mean I like adding to the list."

The drop point was on the far eastern ridge, where the cliffs met a frozen sea. Freija piloted, guiding it low through the jagged peaks while Kimiko scanned the terrain.

Below, the wilderness was stark and merciless – ice dunes, razor-thin ridges, and valleys filled with cracking glaciers that groaned in protest beneath their own weight. Freija's eyes flicked constantly between the terrain and the control panel.

"Are you sure about this guide?" Kimiko asked again, quieter this time.

"No," Freija replied, "but if Frigid trusts him, I'll follow him into the dark."

Kimiko didn't respond, but the tension in her jaw eased. Outside, the winds howled louder. The charm at her neck vibrated once.

"We're close," she said.

They landed on a narrow ledge beside a jagged cliff, just as the storm began to roll in. Snow churned in the air, visibility dropping fast. Kimiko scanned the area.

The Guide in the Snow

They landed on a narrow ledge beside a jagged cliff, just as the storm began to roll in. Snow churned in the air, visibility dropping fast. Kimiko scanned the area.

Then she saw him – a broad-shouldered figure in fur-lined armor, his face half-concealed by a cowl. The wolf mark on his shoulder was unmistakable.

"You're late," he called over the wind.

"You're cryptic," Freija shot back.

The man trudged forward, boots crunching heavily through the powder. Up close, his armor bore faint sigils etched into the metal beneath the fur lining. His eyes were sharp and gray, scanning them both like a commander assessing a battlefield.

"Kael," he said, offering a curt nod. "Frigid told me to expect two. Didn't say one of them would be a tourist."

Kimiko arched a brow. "Off-worlder, actually. Tourists don't usually come armed."

Kael gave the barest hint of a smirk. "Fair. She said you were quick with a blade. We'll see."

Freija stepped slightly in front of Kimiko. "She's not here to impress anyone. And we don't have time to argue or posture."

26

Kael grunted. "I don't argue or posture. I survive." He turned, gesturing for them to follow. "Let's get out of the open."

They moved toward the base of the cliff, Kael navigating with casual ease despite the deepening snow. As they walked, he spoke just loud enough to carry over the storm.

"I've scouted the entrance. It's intact, but the runes are active again. And not in any pattern I recognize. It's like something stirred them."

Freija glanced toward the mountain wall. "You think it's awake?"

Kael didn't answer immediately. "I think something *else* woke it. That quake didn't just shake loose stone."

Kimiko's hand went to her charm as it gave another faint pulse.

"Let me guess," Kael said. "That thing's been throbbing the closer you got?"

"More like syncing," Kimiko replied.

He nodded. "Then it's responding to whatever's inside. And that means it knows you're here."

They reached the base of the cliff. Snow whirled around them in tight eddies, caught in unnatural currents.

Kael placed his gloved hand against a seam in the stone. "Entrance is just ahead. But before we go in... understand something."

Freija raised a brow.

"You're not just walking into a cave. You're stepping into memory. And sometimes, memories bite back."

Kimiko studied him. "You've been in before?"

"Far enough to lose a few things. People. Certainty. That kind of thing." He stepped back, hand still on the wall. "Still want me to guide you?"

Freija didn't hesitate. "Yes."

Kael nodded once. "Then follow me. And remember – don't trust everything you hear in the dark."

Beneath the Ice

The cave swallowed them in stillness. The moment they stepped beyond the rune-inscribed entrance, the air changed; it was thicker, colder, and weighted with a long memory.

Freija took a few steps forward and turned to look back. Her breath curled visibly in the dim light. "I've flown through lightning storms with better lighting."

Kimiko gave her a sideways glance. "You're not exactly building confidence."

"I'm just saying, if anything jumps out at us in here, I get dibs on screaming first."

Kael chuckled under his breath, his voice quieter now. "That's one way to measure courage."

The corridor sloped downward. The walls, though rough in texture, gleamed with veins of crystalized frost. Runes glowed sporadically, reacting to their presence with faint pulses of blue.

"I expected echoes," Kimiko said softly. "But this... it feels like it's listening."

Freija slowed her pace, brushing her fingers along the nearest wall. "It is. You grow up in Icelandia, you learn real quick... our caves don't forget. And they don't always forgive."

Kael pressed ahead, pausing now and then to study the stone. "Some of these formations weren't here last time. The ice is shifting. Reforming."

"Could it be reacting to us?" Kimiko asked.

Kael's tone turned more guarded. "Or to what's waiting deeper in."

They passed a pillar of ice so clear it seemed hollow. Inside, a fossilized feather was suspended mid-air, caught in an eternal drift. Freija stopped to stare.

"This wasn't here before," she murmured.

"Maybe it wanted to be found," Kimiko said.

Freija straightened. "Maybe we weren't supposed to."

The chill deepened. Their charms vibrated once... no pulse, just a tremble like a warning drawn too tight to ignore.

Kael turned. "You feel that?"

Freija nodded. "Something's stirring."

"Then stay sharp," Kael said. "The real welcome starts soon."

Battle with the Wraiths

The cold deepened with every step. A sudden flicker passed through the nearest wall, like the runes themselves were flinching. The light

28

dimmed. The path narrowed. Kimiko's charm vibrated once, and then again… sharper this time.

"Something just shifted," she whispered.

Kael nodded grimly. "This is where it gets worse."

They followed him along a narrow ledge until he paused at a sheer wall.

"This is it."

Freija frowned. "It's solid."

Kael placed his hand on the wall. "Not to those who know where to press."

Kael pushed on a jutting rock. Then the wall shimmered, and a doorway opened – an arch of frost-runes sliding inward with a hiss. Beyond it was only darkness.

Kael lit a red flaming lantern. "You're sure you want this?"

Freija looked to Kimiko. "We came to find answers."

"Then stay behind me," Kael said, stepping into the dark.

The cavern swallowed them whole.

Inside, the temperature dropped sharply. Even Freija felt the sting on her skin, despite her royal Icelandian blood. The walls were smooth ice, etched with runes that glowed faintly as they passed. The tunnel spiraled downward, too clean, too deliberate.

"This wasn't made by nature," Kimiko said quietly.

"No," Kael agreed. "This was carved. Many, many millennia ago."

They walked for what felt like hours, passing beneath archways and through chambers that were too vast to measure. In one, the walls shimmered with frost-locked reflections – fragments of faces, frozen in silent screams.

Kimiko paused. Her charm pulsed twice.

"Movement," she whispered.

Freija ignited her short sword, blades shining with wintry light. "Anyone else feel like this place is alive?"

The shadows stirred. Shapes coalesced in the dark – vague outlines of humanoid figures, their bodies composed of shifting ice and smoke.

"Wraiths," Kael muttered. "Don't let them touch you."

The wraiths charged.

Kimiko drew one out with a sweeping slash, her katana slashing clear through the wraith. The wraith dissolved… then reformed as they recoalesced into their original form.

29

Freija lunged skywards, wings unfurling for a moment before slashing clean through a second. Its body collapsed... but the magical energy swirling in the runes reformed it instantly.

And then they attacked simultaneously, two icy maelstroms converging upon Kimiko and Freija.

Kimiko met one with concerted strength, spinning her blades, each strike precise and lethal. One wraith grasped at her throat; she evaded it with a pirouette.

Freija flipped midair, dagger in one hand. A wraith's arm snapped at her; she blocked and spun, enough to send the creature staggering.

Kael dropped to one knee before a rune circle etched into the floor, his hands tracing the runic symbols. The designs flared.

The wraiths shrieked.

Kimiko shouted, "Now!"

Kael's runes exploded with white-blue frost energy. A shockwave shattered ice crystal wraith forms. The creatures screamed and dispersed... clouds of cold vapor drifting away.

Silence swallowed them.

Freija landed, panting. "What took you so long?"

Kael rose slowly, lantern aloft. His expression was impassive. "Rituals take time."

Kimiko exhaled, touching her pendant. "Our charms... they led us here."

Freija offered a shaky grin. "See? They do more than pulse."

They shared a brief glance. Not warm exactly – but forged.

Kael rose. "We're getting close."

"What's ahead?" Freija asked.

Kael hesitated. "A vault. Something old. Something your father didn't want anyone to find."

The charm around Kimiko's neck pulsed again – this time, three steady beats.

Freija felt it too. Something had awakened.

And it was waiting.

Echoes After the Battle

The wraiths' remnants still drifted like wisps of mist, curling along the edges of the ruined chamber. Kimiko exhaled slowly, gripping one of her katanas in silence, waiting to see if anything else would stir.

Nothing did. Only the cold remained.

Freija lowered her weapon but didn't sheath it. Her wings were half-furled, feathers twitching slightly with residual tension. "That was more than just a defense mechanism. This place isn't trying to keep people out. It's… testing us."

Kael stood at the far edge of the chamber, lantern raised high. "And you passed. For now."

Kimiko turned toward him. "You said the Vault was ahead. What exactly are we walking into?"

Kael hesitated. "There's something ancient buried here. A presence. Maybe a prison. Maybe a gate. No one knows for sure. But the royal line of Icelandia has guarded its secret for generations."

Freija stepped closer to the nearest wall, her hand brushing a relief carving just barely visible through the frost. "Then why keep the map hidden even from us?"

"Because your father feared what lies inside more than who might find it," Kael answered. "He trusted Frigid to watch over the Archives. But he never expected the quake to unseal it."

The room grew quieter. Kimiko's charm pulsed once, then settled again.

Freija broke the tension with a dry laugh. "Next time someone says 'family secrets,' I'm going to think of cursed ice vaults and angry ghosts."

Kimiko raised an eyebrow. "You're already thinking of that now."

"Fair."

Kael started toward the narrow exit opposite where they'd entered. "We'll camp briefly in the next chamber. The Vault isn't far, but getting close will stir the magic again. And we need to be ready."

"Then let's move," Kimiko said. "Before whatever's watching decides to test us again."

The Harbinger Sleeps

Descent Into the Deep

The tunnel spiraled farther below the surface of Mount Solance, the narrow path slick with veins of ancient frost that pulsed faintly beneath the ice. Each step echoed in unsettling rhythm, swallowed seconds later by the silence that pressed around them like a living presence. Their lanterns, Kael's red flame and the twin Frostheart charms, cast glimmers that rebounded off the icy walls in muted halos.

Kimiko moved in silence, her katanas now sheathed but her hand never far from its grip. She could feel something within her shift, not in alarm, but in awareness, as if something familiar stirred beyond the ice. Ahead, Freija led with quiet determination, her breath slow and measured, wings furled tightly behind her. Kael brought up the rear, his boots crunching over frost-laced stone with calm certainty.

"We're deeper than any map ever suggested," Kael said, voice low. "Even the oldest archives don't reach this far."

"Does that worry you?" Kimiko asked without turning.

"It should. But worry won't change what's ahead."

Freija paused at a bend, placing a hand against a frost-veined rune embedded in the wall. The glow pulsed beneath her palm, then faded again.

"Still active," she muttered.

Kael stepped beside her. "Some of these sigils date back to the Time of Sundering. They weren't meant to be disturbed."

Kimiko raised an eyebrow. "Then why keep walking?"

"Because something older than memory is waking," Kael replied. "And I don't think it cares whether we understand it."

The air grew colder as they pressed on, their breaths now thick clouds that hung before them like ghosts. The tunnel opened into a wide, domed cavern, its ceiling rising high above with frozen stalactites gleaming like teeth. At its center, a spiraling column of ice reached from floor to ceiling, etched with ancient sigils that throbbed faintly with pale-blue light.

Kimiko stopped short. "This is it."

Kael nodded solemnly. "The threshold. The Vault lies beyond that wall."

Freija stepped forward, eyes narrowed. "Do you hear that?"

Kimiko strained her senses. At first, there was nothing. Then, barely audible, the sound of slow, labored breathing. It echoed faintly through the chamber, as though the mountain itself exhaled in slumber.

Freija swallowed. "I don't think it's the mountain."

They approached the spiraling column together. As Kael moved his lantern close, the light refracted inside the ice, revealing a shadowy form partially entombed within... a massive, vaguely humanoid, with jagged protrusions like shards of frozen armor jutting from its limbs.

Kimiko's eyes widened. "That's not a statue."

Kael nodded grimly. "Iskarion. The Harbinger. Bound in frost by the ancients. And not as dormant as we hoped."

Freija stared, transfixed. Her charm glowed steadily now, synchronizing with a pulse she couldn't hear but felt deep in her bones. "Why is he still alive?"

Kael's expression tightened. "He's not. Not entirely. But he remembers. And he dreams."

A low groan vibrated through the ice beneath their feet.

Kimiko stepped back instinctively, hand on her weapon. "Do we need to run?"

Kael didn't answer immediately. Then he said, "No. Not yet. But stay alert. The Vault is open because he wants it to be."

Freija looked from the entombed elemental to Kimiko, then back to Kael. "Then let's not keep him waiting."

The Retreat

The groan from beneath the ice grew louder, rising to a deep, echoing rumble that vibrated through the walls of the cavern. Cracks began to spiderweb outward from the frozen column holding Iskarion. The pulse from Kimiko and Freija's Frostheart charms grew erratic.

Kael took one last look at the elemental's hulking shape, now shifting faintly within its icy prison. "We need to move. Now."

Freija turned, her voice low and tense. "He's stirring."

"I thought he was supposed to be dreaming," Kimiko said, eyes locked on the faint movement within the frost.

Kael started back toward the tunnel. "Dreams can turn to waking in an instant. Whatever you just saw, whatever he sensed in us... it's enough. We go."

They moved quickly. Kimiko kept pace beside Freija, her hand resting on the hilt of her katana. "What exactly did we just witness? That didn't feel like a memory."

"It wasn't," Freija said, breath sharp. "He looked right at me. Through the ice. He knew."

Kael's voice cut in from ahead. "Iskarion remembers everything. Every war. Every betrayal. The runes were supposed to hold his mind in stasis, not his body."

"Did we wake him?" Kimiko asked.

"No," Kael said over his shoulder. "We just reminded him he's not alone."

Snow dust flaked down from the ceiling of the tunnel as they ascended, faster now. The air itself seemed to tighten, colder with every breath.

Freija glanced at Kimiko. "Why us? Why now?"

Kimiko shook her head. "Maybe it's the bloodline. Maybe it's the charms. Maybe it is your father's meddling. Or maybe... he's been waiting."

Kael paused at a turning, placing his hand briefly against the wall. The runes beneath his palm flared, then dimmed. He exhaled. "We're still safe. For now."

"Define safe," Freija muttered.

They moved up the corridor in silence for a few moments before Kimiko broke it. "He didn't attack. He could have shattered that ice, reached for us. He didn't."

"That was a warning," Kael said. "He let us see him because he wanted us to carry what we saw."

Freija frowned. "To whom? Frigid? My father?"

"Everyone," Kael replied. "He wants us to tell the world he's still here. And he's listening."

As they reached the last rise before the surface breach, Kimiko slowed, glancing back into the darkness behind them.

"I don't think this is over," she said quietly.

Freija stopped beside her. "It isn't. But we need answers before we come back."

Kael moved past them toward the frozen ledge. The blizzard outside howled against the rock face. "You will come back. When you do, bring more than questions. Bring resolve."

They stepped into the storm, the roar of wind swallowing the last whisper of Iskarion's chamber behind them. The mountain did not speak, but in the pulse of their charms, in the shiver of their breath, they knew the Harbinger was no longer sleeping peacefully.

Shattered Trust

The return to Frostholm was a silent flight, carried on low altitude currents that hissed past the hull of the glide craft. The mountains seemed taller now, the snow heavier, the wind more hostile. Inside the cockpit, Freija sat stiffly at the controls, her jaw tight and her mind storming.

Kimiko sat beside her in silence, her face partially hidden beneath the hood of her cloak. She said nothing, but Freija could feel her presence, attentive and focused. The Frostheart charms at Kimiko's and Freija's necks no longer pulsed, but both of them could still feel the echo of what they had encountered beneath Mount Solance. The Vault. The whispers. The prisoner.

Freija finally spoke, her voice brittle. "I think Frigid's been keeping things from me. Not just protecting our father. She's protecting the whole truth."

Kimiko remained quiet for a moment. "Would she lie to you?"

"She wouldn't lie. But she would withhold," Freija said. "Out of duty. Out of fear. Or because she still believes Father can fix this."

Kimiko gave a slow nod. "Even when silence could cost your kingdom?"

Freija's grip tightened on the controls. "That's what I intend to find out."

Confronting Frigid

They landed quietly in the northern courtyard, far from the official hangars, away from the ever-watching eyes of the guards and Parliament advisors. The sky above them was slate-gray, thick with swirling snow. Frostholm loomed, its spires sharp against the storm.

Freija led the way through a narrow servant's corridor, past shimmering ice walls that reflected their strained expressions. When they reached Frigid's private chamber, a polished, blue-tinged sanctum buried deep in the west wing, Freija didn't knock.

She burst through the door.

Frigid stood near her writing desk, startled but composed as ever. She turned with a measured gaze. "Sister?"

Freija didn't hesitate. "You didn't tell me how bad it was."

Frigid blinked, setting her quill down. "You'll have to be more specific. What did you find?"

Kimiko slipped inside and closed the door silently behind them.

"We found the Vault," Freija said.

That word changed everything.

Frigid's posture tightened. She stepped away from the desk slowly. "You opened it?"

"It opened to us," Freija said. "Because something in it recognized us. Or me. Or him," she added, pointing to a tapestry of their father.

Frigid's lips parted slightly at the gesture. "Him... you mean..."

"Our father," Freija said, her voice low and furious. "He's been feeding it. Empowering whatever lives in that prison. There's a being buried beneath the mountain, Frigid. Alive. Sentient."

Frigid looked down, her hands clasped tightly together. For a long moment, she said nothing. Then she turned and walked to the frostglass window, staring out into the snow.

"You weren't supposed to go that far," she said quietly. "You were supposed to observe. To confirm."

"Confirm what?" Freija asked angrily. "That your instincts were right? That something ancient and malevolent is buried beneath our kingdom and Father's been playing with forces none of us understand?"

Kimiko spoke now, her tone firm. "At what point does honesty to your people outweigh loyalty to your king? If your father is endangering Icecrest, shouldn't protecting the kingdom come first?"

Frigid exhaled and crossed her arms tightly. "Then you understand why Father is doing what he's doing. He's not mad. He's scared."

"He's reckless," Freija shot back. "You didn't see it stir. You didn't feel it breathing. That thing isn't just an echo from the past. It's alive. It's angry. And it's about to wake up!"

Frigid's expression faltered. She moved to the hearth and stared into the pale red-yellow flames. "I never wanted to believe it. I told myself the stories we were fed as children were just frost-folk tales. The Harbinger. The Vault. The War of the Wings. But lately... I've been wondering if our ancestors left more than legends behind."

"You sound like Father," Freija said bitterly. "He used to tell us bedtime stories about winged beasts and sleeping gods. I thought they were just dreams. Now he's waking one up."

"He didn't intend to," Frigid replied sharply. "But something changed. He received a report from Skarae in the East last month, one he hasn't shared with the Parliament. Their outer ridges are under siege."

Kimiko turned slightly, her gaze focused. "From what?"

Frigid hesitated. "They don't know. Entire geothermal cities have gone dark. The magma vents are freezing over. Survivors talk of shapes in the ice. Shadows that whisper. They say it came from beneath."

Freija scoffed. "And now you believe it's connected to some ancient entity our great-great-grandfather sealed away with fairy dust?"

Frigid faced her. "I believe something old is waking up, and that we are not prepared to stop it with frostcraft and diplomacy alone."

Kimiko stepped forward slowly. Her voice was calm, but her eyes sharp. "Tell me the rest. The myths. The parts they left out."

Frigid studied her for a moment, then looked back at Freija. "Do you remember the old scrolls Mother forbade us from reading? The ones kept in the Winter Vault?"

Freija blinked. "You mean the ones written in runes too old for translation?"

Frigid nodded. "They weren't indecipherable. Just dangerous. Father has been spending more time with them. He believes the Harbinger wasn't alone, that other entities were buried across the four continents, each tied to a different elemental force. One for fire. One for stone. One for wind. Ours, for ice."

Freija folded her arms. "And what? You think they're returning?"

"I think they never left," Frigid whispered.

Silence fell. The storm outside intensified, its rhythm a slow, mournful beat against the stained-glass windows.

Kimiko moved closer, her voice low. "If these legends hold any truth, then your father may not be trying to unleash the Harbinger, but to prepare for something worse."

Freija's expression darkened. "That doesn't justify what he's doing."

"No," Frigid agreed. "But it might explain it."

For a long moment, no one spoke.

Then Freija turned to Kimiko. "Do you really believe this?"

"I believe in patterns," Kimiko said. "And right now, the pieces don't add up unless we start looking backward."

Frigid offered her a tight nod. "There's more in the records. I've only scratched the surface."

"Then we dig," Kimiko said simply.

Freija sighed, looking down at the Frostheart pendant that hung from her neck. She touched it absently.

She wanted to trust Frigid again, but something in her heart had shifted. The weight of betrayal, of secrets kept in the name of duty, pressed against her chest. She wasn't sure which hurt more. Frigid's silence, or the realization that their father had never stopped playing god.

"If the past is coming back," she said quietly, "then we better make sure we understand it before it swallows us."

Outside, the wind howled. And deep beneath the ice, something also listened.

The Forbidden Records

Frostholm's Winter Vault was older than the palace itself – carved into the mountain when Icelandia was still a fractured world, before the First Accord, before the Parliament, before even the crown was forged.

Frigid led Freija and Kimiko down into its depths, the only sound their boots echoing softly along frost-hardened stone. The corridor walls shimmered with enchanted runes, faintly glowing with residual magic. It was said the vault could repel all forms of corruption – though none of them were certain that was still true.

They descended until the air grew dense and quiet. The final door bore no handle, only a sunburst rune carved in faded silver. Frigid touched her palm to it, and the stone shifted inward, granting them entry.

Inside was a long, low room lit by glacial lanterns. Rows of stone pedestals cradled scrolls, tomes, and tablets from ages long forgotten. Dust hung in the air like fog. It felt like entering a tomb – not of bodies, but of memory and history.

"These were locked away after the Unification," Frigid said quietly. "Parliament forbade their study. Too dangerous. Too wild. But Father has been coming here, reading them in secret."

Freija approached a table stacked with age-darkened scrolls. "This doesn't feel like stories anymore."

"It's not," Kimiko said, her voice level. "It is history buried beneath belief."

Frigid pulled one scroll from the stack and carefully unfurled it across a reading slab. The image it revealed was richly detailed – four massive beings, each towering over a distinct landscape.

One was wreathed in flame, its body molten and crowned with smoke. It stood atop volcanic peaks – **Skarae**.

Another was of stone and earth, limbs like crags, rising from a canyon plateau – **Sommara**.

A third flew on gusts of wind, its form shifting, faceless, surrounded by clouds and sky spires – **Dorland**.

The fourth was unmistakable: carved of ice, jagged and beautiful, with wings like frozen glass. It hovered above a spire – **Icecrest**.

"This scroll predates the Parliament by centuries," Frigid murmured. "It tells of the four Elementals – sentient beings tied to the essence of each continent. Some believe they shaped the continents themselves."

"And that they went to war," Freija added grimly.

Kimiko stepped closer, examining the symbols encircling each elemental. "They weren't just beings of power. They were worshipped. Feared. Possibly even obeyed."

Frigid opened a second scroll. This one depicted battle: the elementals clashing, tearing across the world in storms and quakes. But what caught their eyes was what came next – a great convergence, a circle formed by mages and warriors of all four continents, chaining the Elementals in place.

"And then they were sealed," Frigid said. "Each continent took responsibility for its own. The pact was forged in blood, ice, and magic."

"But ours was different," Freija said, pointing to the third scroll Frigid unfurled.

This one was darker, more abstract. The frost elemental – The Harbinger – was shown towering over the others, consuming the sky itself. Around it stood Icelandian figures bowing… and one standing alone, a figure haloed in light, holding a strange shape in its hands.

Kimiko tilted her head. "What is that?"

Frigid shook her head. "We don't know. Some scholars believed it was a Vessel. Others, a seal. But look here…"

She tapped the edge of the scroll, where the faded script curved in a spiral. "The name is unreadable. The ink has degraded, or perhaps it was never meant to be spoken."

Freija frowned. "It looks like a person, not an elemental."

"Yes," Frigid said. "Some scrolls speak of a fifth figure with blue skin and wings fully extended – different from the elemental forces. A balance. A gatekeeper."

Kimiko's eyes narrowed. "Not born of fire, stone, air, or frost. But of... will. Of heart."

Frigid looked at her in surprise.

"It's in the posture," Kimiko explained. "That's a warrior's stance. One who protects. Not one who commands."

Freija's brow furrowed. "Then why was this never told? Why leave this out of the fairy tales?"

"Because the Gatekeeper couldn't be summoned," Frigid said. "They had to be found. Chosen. Their soul had to align with the essence of harmony itself. The others were unleashed through arcane rituals. But this one... they were born."

"And lost," Kimiko murmured. "Or buried."

Frigid unrolled another scroll. This one was incomplete – burned at the edges. It showed only the Gatekeeper's silhouette standing before the frost elemental, arms raised and wings nearly fully unfurled, while the other three elementals stood behind it. The final symbol at the scroll's bottom was almost illegible.

"This is what Father's been chasing," Frigid said softly. "He believes this figure can control or bind the Harbinger."

Freija scowled. "And in trying to find them, he's been reawakening the Harbinger."

"The seal was never stable," Frigid said. "But his search has accelerated its weakening."

Kimiko stepped back from the table, her expression unreadable. "He's looking for salvation. But he's feeding destruction."

Silence fell over them again.

Freija finally broke it. "If this Gatekeeper was real, and if they're more than just a fable – how do we find them?"

Frigid closed the scroll gently. "I don't know. But there may be more answers in the ruins near Mount Solance. That's where the first binding took place. And the only place the seal might still remember."

Kimiko looked down at the scroll again, at the symbol etched beneath the Gatekeeper's feet.

"Then we go," she said.

And high above the chamber, unseen by mortal eyes, the Frostheart charms glowed faintly in rhythm.

The Gatekeeper's legend had returned.

And Icelandia was listening.

Echoes of the Past

Reckonings Beneath the Snow

The mountain winds sang a dirge as the trio emerged from the depths of the Winter Vault. Snow swirled through the high corridors, carried in through cracked windows and narrow vents, as if the palace itself was exhaling centuries of silence. They said little as they returned to Frigid's chambers, each carrying the weight of what they had read.

Frigid stood near the hearth, staring into the fire, her expression unreadable.

"I never believed any of it," she said finally. "The stories of the Elementals, yes – those were childhood tales, myths to keep us respectful of the old ways. But the Gatekeeper... I'd never heard that name spoken in anything other than riddles or broken verses."

Freija pulled her frost-lined cloak tighter around her shoulders. "You mean to say you didn't think it was real until now?"

Frigid nodded slowly. "Not really. The concept of a fifth force, a balance to the chaos – it sounded too poetic. Too neat. Our tutors barely touched on it. Even the archives only referred to it in passing. I thought it was just a metaphor, or some embellishment added centuries later."

Kimiko stepped forward. "But now you've seen the scrolls. You know it wasn't fiction. Someone witnessed that figure, and the seal. The details are too precise to be a fabrication."

Frigid exhaled. "I'm still trying to process it. The idea that a person – not a spell, not a weapon – was once able to stand before the Elementals and bring them to a halt... it reshapes everything we've believed."

"It reshapes everything you were taught to believe," Freija said, a note of frustration in her voice. "While Father was down in those vaults, learning the truth, we were raised on half-truths and shadows."

Frigid turned toward her sister. "I didn't know he was reading them. Not until recently. And even then, he didn't share everything."

"That's the problem," Freija snapped. "He kept us in the dark. You kept me in the dark. If we are to protect Icecrest, we need truth – not caution and secrets."

Kimiko raised a calming hand. "Maybe this is the time to share, then. All of it. Because what we saw down there changes how we move forward."

Frigid's shoulders sank slightly, her voice low. "I agree. No more secrets. We follow this trail. All of us."

Freija leaned against the frosted stone archway, her wings curled tightly around her shoulders. "But now we have to figure out what Father's actually been trying to do – and what he might have already awakened."

Frigid turned to them. "Then we need someone who understands the old magic better than any of us. Someone who remembers the world before the Parliament tried to bury it."

Freija raised an eyebrow. "You're talking about the Seer?"

Frigid nodded. "Her name is Lysari. She lives in exile in the Cradle of Silence – an old observatory turned shrine near the edge of the northern ice shelf. The Parliament exiled her decades ago for warning of 'the frost beyond frost.' I think she's been watching all this unfold long before we knew it was happening."

"Is she sane?" Freija asked.

Frigid gave a wry smile. "More than most of the people still in power."

The Seer in the Snow

In the following morning, they made preparations quickly. Kael returned with supplies and armor reinforced with enchantments and loaded them into a 6-person glide craft. Despite the storm's rising fury, they set out before dawn, guided by Frigid's old maps and Kael's instincts.

The journey to the Cradle of Silence took them along the high ridges of the Serac Range – sheer cliffs of ancient ice, sculpted by millennia of wind. The skies above churned with slow-moving auroras, and far below, the frost-sunken valleys glowed with unnatural light.

As they traveled, Kimiko grew more reflective. The scrolls haunted her. The image of the Icelandic Gatekeeper – unreadable, unnamed, but unmistakably purposeful – lingered in her mind. The Frostheart charm at her neck pulsed occasionally, almost in rhythm with her breath.

They reached the observatory at twilight. A stone tower stood like a shard of obsidian buried in ice, half-collapsed and weather worn. Runes were carved into the outer walls, flickering faintly with residual magic.

Lysari waited by the broken gate.

She was small, hunched beneath layers of fur-lined robes, her face partially veiled. Her wings looked old and had a few missing feathers. But her eyes – silver and sharp as a dagger's edge – missed nothing. She studied them each in turn.

"I wondered when the daughters of frost would come," she said.

"You know who we are?" Freija asked, stepping forward.

"I knew who you would be," Lysari replied, and then turned her eyes to Kimiko. "But you... I did not expect you so soon."

Kimiko held her gaze, unflinching. "We need answers. About the Harbinger. About the Gatekeeper."

Lysari turned and began walking toward the observatory. "Then come. The frost remembers. And it has waited a long time to be heard."

Inside, the chamber was half-collapsed but preserved through spells that clung like cobwebs. The inner sanctum was circular, with a domed ceiling etched in runes of the four continents. At the center stood a frozen pedestal, and upon it, a crystal sphere glowing faintly blue.

Lysari placed her hands on the sphere.

"The Harbinger is not bound by ice alone. Its roots stretch through memory, through the fear etched into your bloodlines. It was never just a weapon – it was a mirror of ambition. That's why your father cannot control it. He stokes it, not out of malice, but desperation."

Freija stepped forward. "Then what about the Gatekeeper? Is it real?"

Lysari looked to her. "It is more than real. It is necessary. The Gatekeeper was not made by magic but chosen by harmony. Where the others represent force, it represents balance. Its power does not destroy, but binds."

Kimiko's heart raced, though she kept her face unreadable.

"Do you know where to find them?" Frigid asked.

Lysari slowly shook her head. "No. Because they are not buried. They are not summoned. They must be awakened. And only when the world needs them most."

Freija frowned. "Then how do we prepare?"

Lysari raised a hand to the ceiling. The runes began to shimmer with light – each representing the four elemental forces. Then a fifth symbol appeared in the center, glowing with golden white light. It was the same symbol from the scroll.

"The Gatekeeper will rise not where power gathers, but where sacrifice is offered. They will come when the heart outweighs fear. But their strength cannot act alone. The Gatekeeper's spirit must bind with one of royal blood, someone who bears the lineage of leadership, but more importantly, a heart shaped by duty and compassion. A Vessel."

Freija glanced down at her Frostheart charm, feeling its warmth pulse again.

Frigid's eyes narrowed. "So the Gatekeeper is not a person... but a presence?"

"A consciousness," Lysari said. "One that needs an anchor. A soul strong enough to wield its wisdom and endure its weight."

Freija's voice was tight. "Then Father's search may have doomed us. He looked for the Gatekeeper with the mind of a conqueror, not the heart of a protector."

They stood in silence.

Outside, the auroras swirled in haunting spirals above the northern sky. The wind had stilled, just briefly, as if the world itself was listening.

And far beneath the ice, the Harbinger stirred.

A Queen's Doubt

The wind screamed across the Serac Range as the group descended from the Cradle of Silence, leaving Lysari's shrine behind. Though the sun usually stayed low on the horizon during the early Spring days on Icelandia, a pale silvery light shimmered through the clouds, casting everything in a muted glow. The journey back was somber. No one spoke.

Back in Frostholm, the palace guards greeted their return with quiet bows but curious eyes. Kael took their gear to be cleaned and refitted, while Frigid led Freija and Kimiko directly to her chambers, bypassing the throne hall entirely.

The moment the door sealed behind them, Freija exhaled sharply and threw her coat over a frost-carved chair. "That woman knew too much."

Frigid unpinned her cloak and let it slide to the floor. "She always did. That's why they exiled her."

Kimiko sat on the edge of the crystal bench near the hearth, watching the fire flicker light against the ice walls. Her Frostheart charm pulsed gently against her chest, steady as a heartbeat.

Freija also noticing her Frostheart charm pulsating frustratingly said, "She confirmed it. The Gatekeeper exists. And it needs a Vessel."

Frigid nodded. "One of royal blood. With the heart of a protector."

Freija crossed her arms. "Which could mean either of us."

Silence lingered, thick and heavy.

Freija broke it with a firm tone. "We have to tell Mother."

Frigid looked away. "She doesn't need to be pulled into this yet. Not until we know more."

"She's the Queen, Frigid," Freija snapped angrily. "And our mother. If she doesn't know what Father's doing, then she's in just as much danger as the rest of us."

Frigid's jaw clenched tightly, "Or she does know and is staying silent for a reason. You want to tear open family loyalties on a hunch, Freija?"

"It's not a hunch," Freija said sharply. "We've seen it. Heard it. And if you really think she's the type to ignore the truth."

"I don't know what I think!" Frigid snapped, voice louder than she intended with her wings extending more than half unfurled. She paused, took a breath, then added more quietly, "I don't know what to believe anymore."

Kimiko spoke gently. "On Earth… or at least where I'm from, keeping secrets from family is usually a sign of distrust. But here, among royalty, I've noticed it's more… common. Expected, even."

Freija gave a wry smile. "You're not wrong."

Kimiko continued, "Still, if the Gatekeeper is real, and if your father is trying to awaken the Harbinger… isn't it worse to leave the Queen in the dark? At least give her the choice to act."

Frigid's shoulders sagged. "You're both right. We need her. If she's not involved, then she's the only one who can help us."

Kimiko stood. "Then let's speak to her. Now."

Frigid sighed, rubbing her temples. "I can't believe I'm taking advice from my younger sister."

Freija grinned. "It's only by ten minutes!"

Meeting with Mother Queen

Queen Glaciana's private sanctum was in the eastern wing, beyond the Parliament chambers. Freija hadn't stepped foot inside in years – long before joining the Crimson Alliance. The hallway that led to her doors was lined with frostglass panels that glowed softly in her presence.

When they entered, the Queen was seated beside a suspended garden of snow-blooming orchids, her hands folded delicately in her lap. She wore robes of midnight blue and glacial silver, and a soft crown rested upon her brow. At least four advisors and two record-keepers stood nearby, consulting runes on glowing scrolls.

Freija stepped forward immediately. "Mother, we need to speak to you. Privately."

Glaciana raised an eyebrow, then dismissed the attendants with a graceful wave of her hand. They left without protest, and the chamber door was sealed behind them.

"What troubles you?" Glaciana asked.

Frigid didn't hesitate. "It's Father. He's been using ancient scrolls, drawing power from things sealed long ago beneath Mount Solance. He's trying to find the Gatekeeper."

"The Gatekeeper?" the Queen echoed, voice unreadable.

Freija moved beside her sister. "We thought it was a myth. But it's not. The scrolls describe four elemental forces buried across the world... and a fifth, meant to bind them. The Gatekeeper. They're real. And the scrolls spoke of the Vessel – the one who must carry the Gatekeeper's spirit."

Kimiko added, "And we've seen one. The Harbinger of Ice, buried deep beneath Mount Solance. We entered the Vault. We saw the conduits, the seals, and the pulse of something ancient... angry and aware. We barely escaped."

Freija stepped forward again, her voice sharp. "Father is awakening it. Feeding it power. But the Gatekeeper isn't just a solution to that... it's the balance to all four. And it needs someone of royal blood... our royal blood," she said pointing to her and Frigid. "Someone chosen. That's what the Vessel is."

"I used to tell you those stories when you were little," Glaciana said quietly. "Tales of balance, of the four great powers and the one who would unify them. I called him the Light in the Storm."

Freija nodded. "We remember."

"But they were just stories," Glaciana continued. "Allegories. Teachings wrapped in myth."

Frigid stepped closer. "They're not stories. They're real. The figures on the scrolls match the statues in the vault. The runes... the seals... they weren't just symbolic. They were protective. And they're weakening."

Kimiko's voice was calm but resolute. "Even on Earth, many of our myths have roots in truth. Legends passed down, generation by generation, between parent and child. Just because something is old doesn't mean it isn't real."

Glaciana studied their faces, her expression softening with concern. Her gaze dropped to the Frostheart charms at their necks. Kimiko's glowed faintly, slow and serene. Freija's pulsed brighter, faster... almost in rhythm with her quickening breath.

Frigid retrieved a copied scroll and placed it on the table. "This is what we found. The Gatekeeper surrounded by the four Elementals. And more than that... a fifth symbol, center and radiant."

"You believe you've been chosen?" Glaciana asked softly.

"No," Freija said. "But someone will be. The Vessel isn't random. It's someone with both legacy and heart. We're not here asking you to name one of us. We're asking you to help us stop what's coming."

Glaciana's eyes shimmered faintly, the only sign of emotion on her otherwise calm face. "Even if I believe you, what can I do?"

"Open the sealed records. Let us see what the Parliament buried. Let us find the truth together," Frigid said.

Glaciana turned to the frostglass window, silent for a long moment.

"I… will consider it."

Disappointment flickered across Frigid's face, but she didn't argue. "Then at least speak with Father. Watch him. You'll see."

Glaciana finally nodded. "Very well. I'll summon him for a private audience tonight."

As the trio turned to leave, the Queen called softly, "Freija."

She stopped.

Glaciana approached her and laid a hand gently on her shoulder. "Be careful. Your father is not the man he once was. But he is still the man I love."

Freija nodded, throat tight. "I'll be careful."

They left the Queen's chamber in silence, the snow falling heavier outside the high windows.

In the distance, the Vault pulsed once more, unseen, beneath layers of time and ice.

The Twins Confide

The moonlight over Frostholm cast a pale shimmer across the city, painting the spires and bridges in ghostly hues. The storm had eased, leaving behind a pristine stillness that blanketed the palace in fragile silence. Inside the western wing, Freija's chamber was dimly lit by the flicker of hearth light. Soft frost danced along the high-arched windows as the wind whispered lullabies against the glass.

Frigid stood by the window, arms folded, wings tucked tight against her back. She stared out into the vastness of the capital, silent and composed, her face unreadable. Freija lay on the velvet daybed nearby, her boots discarded and one wing draped lazily over the edge. Her short white hair was tousled, her expression uncharacteristically somber.

"I miss when things made sense," Freija muttered.

Frigid didn't turn. "Did they ever?"

Freija smirked faintly. "Good point. But at least they used to pretend better."

A long silence stretched between them. Outside, the auroras shimmered faintly above the city, casting rippling bands of light through the frostglass. Kimiko wasn't present – having gone for a midnight walk through the palace's quieter halls – but her presence still lingered in the room like a sharp echo.

"She doesn't sleep much," Frigid said softly, finally breaking the silence.

"Kimiko?" Freija asked, sitting up.

Frigid nodded. "She's always alert. Watching. Like she's waiting for the floor to give way beneath her."

Freija looked down at the Frostheart charm resting on her chest. "She's been through things we can't imagine. I brought her here to get away from all that. To give her something peaceful for once."

Frigid turned to face her, her voice gentle. "You call this peaceful?"

Freija gave a tired laugh, resting her chin in her hand. "It was supposed to be. I imagined long flights over the Skyrime Peaks, introducing her to fire-cider and ice-bread. Showing her the Moonlit Falls. All the places I loved when we were younger."

Frigid moved across the room and sat beside her sister on the edge of the daybed. "You still think of those places like they belong to us."

"They do," Freija said. "Even if everything else changes."

Another pause. The fire popped softly, casting flickers of golden warmth against the blue tones of the walls.

Frigid glanced sideways. "You and Kimiko. There's something deep there."

Freija looked surprised, then quickly shook her head. "Not like that. She and I – we're not... in love, if that's what you're asking."

Frigid raised a brow. "I wasn't asking, exactly. But you're close. Closer than I've seen you with anyone."

Freija exhaled slowly. "She's my teammate. My partner. My friend. We fought side by side during the darkest moments of the war. I remember one time when she was captured by the enemy. When I saw her turn the corner passing a large hill... I... I was so thrilled to see her alive and mostly well. I gave her the biggest hug. There were even times when it felt like the galaxy was burning down around us, and she'd be the one standing beside me. Not saying a word. Just there. Reliable. Steady."

Frigid listened quietly.

"We bled together," Freija continued. "Saved each other more times than I can count. I trust her more than anyone besides you. Maybe even more than myself some days."

Frigid softened. "That kind of loyalty... it's rare."

Freija leaned back, staring at the ceiling. "It's not just loyalty. It's respect. We've seen each other at our worst – exhausted, broken, bleeding – and still believed in each other. You don't come out of that without forging something unshakable."

Frigid's eyes fell to her lap. "You're lucky. To have someone like that."

Freija blinked. "You have me."

Frigid's lips curled slightly. "Always."

A moment passed. Then Frigid reached over and took Freija's hand. "I don't say it enough, but I'm proud of you. You left our world, our safety, and chose to fight for something bigger. I stayed here, buried under protocol and Parliament debates. Sometimes I wonder who made the wiser choice."

Freija squeezed her hand gently. "You did what you were born to do. I did what I had to do. That's the difference."

Frigid chuckled faintly. "You always make it sound so simple."

"It's not," Freija admitted. "But it keeps me sane to think of it that way."

The door opened quietly, and Kimiko stepped inside. Her cloak was dusted with snow, her eyes thoughtful.

"Sorry," she said. "Didn't mean to interrupt."

"You're not," Frigid said, releasing her sister's hand and standing.

Freija gestured toward the fire. "We were just trading memories."

Kimiko gave a faint smile. "Any good ones?"

Freija chuckled. "Still waiting on those."

Kimiko stepped closer to the hearth and warmed her hands. "There's tension in the air. The guards are restless. Something's shifting."

Frigid nodded. "We've felt it too. The Vault stirs. The Parliament pretends it doesn't. And our father walks with shadows."

Kimiko looked at them both. "Then we move forward carefully. Together."

Freija stood and joined her. "No more fairy tales. Just truth."

Frigid gave a single nod. "Truth and frost. It's all we've ever known."

As the three women stood around the fire, the silence between them was no longer heavy – but shared. Trust pulsed in the quiet space between words, as steady and real as the frost beneath their feet.

Something was changing.

And it was only the beginning.

The King's Mandate

The morning sun cast pale, horizontal bands of light through the arched frostglass windows of Queen Glaciana's private chamber. Steam curled gently from a kettle on the hearth, perfuming the air with hints of glacier mint and silver tea bark. For all its serenity, the room felt tighter than usual – smaller. As if the ice itself was eavesdropping.

Queen Glaciana stood near the fire, her long blue-and-silver robes trailing behind her like frozen water. Her wings were resting casually on her back. She did not sip her tea. She didn't need warmth. She needed answers.

The doors opened with a soft, enchanted chime, and King Frostran entered alone, without an escort. His dark ceremonial robes swept the floor, lined with shimmering runes of the old tongue. His expression was calm – too calm.

"Glaciana," he greeted simply.

"Thank you for coming, Frostran," she said, her voice neutral. "We need to speak."

Frostran closed the doors behind him with a wave of his hand, invoking a sealing rune. "I assumed we might."

She turned to face him. "I know you've been spending more time beneath the palace. I've seen the servants whispering. And I've noticed the tremors."

"They're natural," Frostran replied smoothly.

Her eyes narrowed. "No, they're not. Nothing about this is natural anymore. And you know it."

Frostran moved to the center of the room and clasped his hands behind his back. "What is it you want to know, exactly?"

"The truth," she said. "Not the Parliament's version. Not the one you've crafted to keep your advisor's calm. I want to know what's happening across our planet – and why our daughters have returned home to walk a line between myth and madness."

He regarded her quietly for a moment. Then, with an exhale, he nodded.

"Very well. The truth, then," he said.

He walked to the frostglass window and looked out across Frostholm. His tone lowered.

"I've been receiving reports for nearly a year – subtle at first, then impossible to ignore. Something is happening on every continent. Dorland traders reported windstorms of incredible magnitude like hurricanes wiping out crops and wildlife migrating in unnatural patterns. Skarae saw a fire storm that raged through townships destroying everything. And in Sommara, quakes that shook so hard that entire buildings collapsed."

Glaciana's eyes widened. "You never brought this to the Parliament?"

"I couldn't," he said sharply. "Not without certainty. Not without solutions. They would have panicked – or worse, blamed each other. And if you remember, we are not far from civil tensions resurfacing between the regions. It took our ancestors centuries to unify these lands. One crack in that illusion of stability, and we may never reclaim it."

"So, you kept it quiet," she said bitterly.

"I kept it contained," Frostran corrected.

"And what's your solution?" she demanded. "Ancient scrolls? Forbidden rites? Our people are frightened, and your answer is to dive into old magic that was buried… and sealed… for a reason?"

Frostran turned to face her fully. His eyes burned – not with rage, but conviction. "They weren't buried to be forgotten. They were buried to be protected. Hidden until needed again. The four elemental forces were not just legends, Glaciana. They are real. And they are stirring across the entire planet. On all four continents, including our own."

She moved toward him, voice low. "You think you can control them?"

"I don't want to control them," he said. "I want to stop them."

Glaciana froze.

Frostran paced slowly. "The Harbinger below Mount Solance is only one of them. The others are awakening across the continents, drawn by the instability, by the weakening of the seals our ancestors placed. I have seen the signs in the runes, in the quake patterns, in the ice dreams passed down through the bloodline."

She stared at him in disbelief. "The Gatekeeper...?"

He nodded. "The one said to hold the balance. The protector between us and elemental annihilation. I've been searching for its path, its resting place. But its energy is too faint – its presence fractured."

Glaciana stepped back, her voice shaking. "And what do you intend to do if you find it?"

Frostran looked at her, unflinching. "Awaken it. Bind it to a Vessel."

Silence fell.

"A Vessel?" she repeated. "You speak as if it's... an artifact. A weapon. Not a person."

"It must bind with someone of royal blood," he said calmly. "The scrolls are clear. The bloodline must be pure. And the heart must be willing."

Glaciana's voice dropped to a whisper. "You mean to use one of our daughters?"

Frostran did not answer.

"No," she said, firmer. "Absolutely not!" Glaciana turned away and took a few steps toward a window her back to him.

Frostran's expression didn't change. "There is no other way."

"You would sacrifice them?" Glaciana's voice cracked. "For a myth? For some old ghost of a prophecy?"

"It is not a myth," he said, voice rising, stepping toward and placing a hand on her shoulder, turning her back to face him. "It is happening. Right now. And if we do nothing – if we cower behind pretty speeches and ceremonial crowns – then we will not have a kingdom to rule."

Glaciana stepped closer. "You raised them to lead, not to die."

"They wouldn't die," he said. "The Vessel lives. It becomes the Gatekeeper's arm in the world. A guardian. A protector of the realm."

"But they will not be themselves anymore," she replied. "You know what possession does, Frostran. You know what you're asking of them."

He looked away.

Glaciana's breath caught. "You've already chosen, haven't you?"

59

Frostran turned slowly. "Frigid. She's disciplined. Devoted. She's studied the traditions. She understands duty."

"She's a child!" Glaciana shouted.

"She's a woman of the crown," he snapped back. "And Freija was off world for nearly a year. Unreachable. We didn't even know if she would return. This isn't about favoritism. It's about necessity."

"You should have told me," she whispered.

"I didn't want to burden you."

"Don't lie to me." Her eyes burned. "You wanted to do this without interference. Without resistance. Without a mother's grief."

Frostran's shoulders fell slightly, the weight of his decisions finally pressing into him. "Glaciana, I do this not out of cruelty, but love. I would burn my own name from history to spare our people the suffering I've seen in my dreams. I would risk anything!"

"Except your own life," she cut in.

That silenced him.

For a long moment, neither spoke.

Finally, Frostran's voice softened. "I am King. I carry the burden of this world on my back. If I could bear the bond myself, I would. But the Gatekeeper chooses only through lineage. Only through hearts it deems pure."

Glaciana's gaze shimmered, though no tears fell. "And if neither daughter accepts?"

"They must," Frostran demanded. "Because if they don't, the Harbinger will rise unchallenged. And Icecrest and eventually the world will fall to ice and ruin."

He walked past her, toward the door.

"What will you do?" she asked.

He paused, placing a hand on the sealing rune.

"I will speak with Frigid again. Soon," he said though something in his eyes briefly faltered. "I believe she's beginning to understand."

With that, he left her chamber, the door closing behind him with a hiss of magic and frost.

Glaciana remained motionless in the dim light, her breath the only sound.

The Queen of Icelandia stood alone.

And for the first time in many years, she feared her throne could not shield her family from what was coming.

Shadows Stirring

Echoes from the Caves

The warning came at dawn.

A deep, grinding sound like a glacier splitting echoed across the northern highlands. It rippled through the bones of Frostholm itself, awakening the capital in a chorus of alarmed whispers and hurried footfalls. Atop the eastern parapet, Freija stood with her wings partially flared, her eyes locked on the jagged horizon.

"There," Freija said, pointing toward the edge of the Serac Range.

Kimiko adjusted the lenses on a borrowed scout scope and peered through. A column of smoke rose into the twilight-blue sky, but it wasn't fire. It twisted like mist, shimmering with flecks of violet and silver. Even from a distance, it radiated unnatural energy.

"That's coming from the cave system below Mount Vharax," Frigid said.

Kimiko turned her scope to the area and then lowered the scope. "Isn't that where one of the sealed crypts was rumored to be?"

Frigid stepped beside them, her breath forming sharp crystals in the air. "It was just a myth. A burial mound for frost giants, if the old records are to be believed. But no one's set foot near it in generations."

Freija frowned. "Then why is it active now?"

As if in answer, the ground trembled beneath their feet. Snow cascaded from the towers and ramparts. Somewhere in the lower city, a bell tolled in warning. The Frostheart charms at both Kimiko's and

Freija's necks pulsed in unison – steady, cold beats like the echo of a heart trapped beneath the ice.

"It's the same kind of energy we felt in the Vault," Kimiko said.

"Then it's spreading," Freija muttered. "The Harbinger's influence... or something worse."

A knock came at her door. Frigid opened the door to see a messenger. "The Queen is asking for your and Princess Freija's attendance now in the Queen's chambers." The messenger turned and made his way down the hallway.

Freija instantly inquired, "What was that all about?"

"Mother seeks our company, immediately in her chambers."

Freija replied, "Let's go. Kimiko you come too."

Frigid turned, moved to the door and started down the hallway. "When we meet Mother we need to tell her that the activity is expanding into new crypts, it means the seals are escalating faster than expected.."

The Queen's Assembly

Queen Glaciana's private chambers had never hosted a Parliament session before. But with tensions rising and formalities too slow to serve, she had summoned representatives from each continent for a quiet emergency council. Only those she trusted implicitly.

A polished table of frozen Silverwood occupied the center of the room, its surface inlaid with magical veins that shimmered in response to strong emotion. Seated at its edge were four key figures:

- High Envoy Drellis of Dorland from the south, a tall woman with silver-plated armor and a scar that ran from temple to jaw.
- Minister Oruan of Skarae in the east, short and wiry with sunburned skin and sharp eyes.
- Stonewarden Caelric of Sommara in the west, broad and weathered like the mountains he called home.
- Princess Frigid, standing in place of the absent King for Icecrest.

Queen Glaciana stood at the head, her expression a blend of composed regality and barely contained concern. Freija and Kimiko stood quietly off to Glaciana's left, honored guests turned unofficial advisors.

"I thank you for coming on such short notice," Glaciana began. "This council is not official. No scribes. No recorders. Only truth."

Drellis leaned forward. "Then speak it, Your Majesty. The Southern winds have turned chaotic. We lost an entire farming valley to airborne storms last week."

"The East is burning," Oruan said. "Literal fire from the skies. Crops turned to ash. Rivers boiling. I thought it was sabotage. Now I'm not so sure."

Caelric nodded grimly. "And the Western ridge has collapsed in on itself. Three towns are lost. The land won't stop shaking."

The Queen nodded. "You see, then, why I've called you here. These aren't isolated disasters. They are symptoms of something deeper. Something old."

Frigid stepped forward, placing a frostglass scroll on the table. "This is a reproduction of the scroll we recovered from the forbidden archives. It speaks of four elemental forces; each sealed beneath the continents in ancient times."

"Fairy tales," Oruan muttered.

"Once, I thought so too," Frigid said, her voice cool but steady. "Until the Vault beneath Mount Solance opened. Until these two," pointing to Freija and Kimiko, "saw what my father has awakened."

Gasps swept the table. Drellis narrowed her eyes. "Are you saying the King is behind this?"

"Not directly," Glaciana said. "But his actions have stirred the Harbinger. He believes the solution lies in awakening a fifth elemental spirit – the Gatekeeper."

Caelric frowned. "That name appears in our mountain lore. The Heart of Duty. The Guardian Between. But we assumed it was metaphor – a fairy tale we tell our children."

Kimiko spoke softly. "It isn't. We found its symbol. It's story. It was meant to bind the others. To keep the world in balance."

Oruan raised an eyebrow. "And where is this Gatekeeper now?"

Freija crossed her arms. "Lost. Sleeping. Perhaps scattered across spirit and time. My father thinks he can force it back into being. He plans to use one of us to do it."

"One of you?" Drellis asked.

Frigid hesitated. "Only someone of royal blood can serve as the Vessel."

The room fell into tense silence.

Caelric looked to Glaciana. "And do you support this plan?"

The Queen's voice wavered for the first time. "I do not. But I fear it may already be too late. The seals are weakening. The elementals are rising. If we do not find the true Gatekeeper... this world may tear itself apart."

Kimiko stepped forward, her Frostheart charm glowing faintly. "Then we need time. Time to search, to study, to act without being forced into choices we can't undo."

Drellis sighed, sitting back in her chair. "Then let us buy time. Delay the King's plan. Protect the heir. And uncover the truth."

Glaciana gave a single nod. "Then this unofficial council is in agreement. We act in secret. We will seek the Gatekeeper. And we do not tell Frostran until we must."

The Silverwood table pulsed softly beneath their hands. A pact sealed in silence.

Outside the chamber, the wind howled across the ice building with intensity.

The Queen's Resolve

The frostglass doors had barely closed behind the departing envoys when Queen Glaciana raised a hand to pause her daughters. The tension in the chamber clung to the air like unspoken grief, dense and frigid. The room had witnessed a private rebellion, sealed in silence, and now the Queen wanted more than words – she wanted answers.

Kimiko turned toward Freija and the Queen, then gave a respectful bow. Turning toward Freija and saying softly voice carefully indicating that she was not trying to intrude, "I will return to your chambers. This is a matter for family."

Freija gave her a grateful nod, touched by her quiet intuition. Kimiko slipped from the room without another word, her shadow vanishing into the hall like a memory.

For a long moment, only silence remained.

Glaciana moved to the Silverwood table, where the fading glow of the elemental pact shimmered faintly. Her fingers hovered over it, then curled into a trembling fist. She did not speak until the weight of expectation grew unbearable.

"Frigid, you were brave today," she said, her voice thin but composed. "To confront the Parliament. To speak of ancient powers in a time where fear and memory arc becoming indistinguishable."

Freija, arms folded, leaned against the frost-carved wall, her expression taut. "They needed to hear it. If we wait any longer, there might not be anything left to rule."

Frigid stood straighter but did not move. Her eyes, often cold and measured, shimmered with something fragile. "What do we do now,

Mother? What happens if Father declares it – if he demands that I be the Vessel?"

Glaciana looked up sharply. "Then we must decide whether we follow his command... or defy it."

Freija blinked in disbelief. "You would stand against him?"

"I would protect my daughters," Glaciana said, each word weighed with pain. "Even from their father."

Frigid's composure cracked. Her voice wavered, her breath shallow. "But... what if he's right? What if the Gatekeeper really is our only hope? The elements – Mother, they're waking. You've seen the tremors. The firestorms. The shifting lands and twisted winds."

Freija pushed off the wall, stepping toward her sister. "That doesn't mean we offer ourselves like sacrificial lambs to a ghost in a scroll. There has to be another way."

Frigid turned on her heel, pacing the room. "You don't understand. I've devoted over a hundred years to upholding the laws, the traditions, the council, the crown. I've believed in the balance we've maintained. And now Father looks to me, the dutiful one, the dependable one, and I – I don't know if I can say 'no'."

She stopped suddenly, her voice rising. "But I don't want to die, Freija! I don't want to lose myself to some ancient power because I was born a few minutes before you!"

Her voice broke, and a sob escaped her lips.

Freija rushed forward and pulled her into a tight embrace. "Then don't. Don't do this. Not for him. Not for duty."

Frigid buried her face into her sister's shoulder, her body trembling. "If I say no... I betray everything I was raised to believe. But if I say yes, I lose myself. There is no good answer."

Freija's voice cracked. Tears welled in her eyes. "I can't lose you. Not after everything. I fought through stars and shadows to come home to you. You're not just my sister. You're half of me."

Glaciana turned away, one hand pressed to her mouth as tears slipped down her cheeks. For all her elegance, all her command, she was a mother now – nothing more, nothing less.

"I never thought we'd come to this," she whispered. "To beg our children not to obey the laws we taught them to respect."

Frigid pulled back from the hug, wiping her eyes. "And yet, what choice do we have? The continent lords are seeing devastation in their own lands. If the elementals truly are waking, then we're running out of time."

Freija turned toward the Queen. "He plans to name Frigid publicly, doesn't he?"

Glaciana nodded slowly. "He believes the Parliament will support him. The moment Frigid accepts the rite, there will be no turning back."

"Then we stop it before it begins," Freija said fiercely. "We find the Gatekeeper's essence first. We understand it – not bind it. We prove there's another way."

Frigid's voice dropped low. "What if we fail? What if he forces the ritual and I…"

"He won't," Glaciana interrupted, stepping forward again. She placed her hand on Frigid's heart. "You are not his to sacrifice. Not unless you give him that right. And I pray you never will."

Frigid looked down, the weight of duty and love tearing at her. "But if it's between me... and the world?"

Freija shook her head. "No. You don't get to ask that. Not yet. Not while we still have time."

The wind shrieked beyond the palace walls.

Glaciana closed her eyes. "Then we do what must be done. We move first. We search. We protect each other… until the end."

Frigid nodded slowly, her voice hoarse. "Together."

Freija took her sister's hand and held it tightly. "Always."

The Queen turned toward the window. The clouds above the Serac Range shifted ominously, and the earth beneath the palace gave a faint rumble.

The four elements stirred.

And Icelandia braced for what would come next.

A Plan in the Snow

The fire in Freija's chambers crackled softly, but even its warmth couldn't touch the chill that clung to the air. The three women sat in a loose circle, cloaked in silence. Frigid's eyes were fixed on the floor, hands clasped tightly in her lap, while Freija leaned against the armrest of a carved chair, her wings partially folded. Kimiko sat cross-legged on a fur-covered bench near the hearth, her eyes steady, listening.

"She cried," Frigid said quietly. "I've never seen Mother cry like that. Not in a hundred years."

Freija gave a slow nod. "She's terrified. Not just of what's coming... but of what Father's willing to sacrifice to stop it."

Kimiko leaned forward. "And you?"

Frigid looked up, her voice brittle. "I don't know. I always thought I'd be ready to do anything for my kingdom. For my people. But this... this isn't just duty. This is extinction. If I say no, I betray everything I've ever stood for. But if I say yes... I might not survive it."

"You won't," Freija said, voice thick with emotion. "Because I know what this thing does to people. I saw what the Harbinger did to the Vault just by being aware. You don't walk away from that kind of power."

Frigid's composure cracked again. "If I refuse... he will name you."

"Then I'll refuse too," Freija said.

"You can't. If I'm cast out by the Parliament, someone will have to take my place. He's King. He doesn't need consent. He only needs tradition."

The silence returned, this time heavier.

Kimiko, fingers lightly touching the Frostheart charm at her neck, finally spoke. "What do you want to do? Not as a princess. Not as a daughter. You, Frigid."

Frigid closed her eyes, tears threatening. "I want to find the Gatekeeper. Before he tries to use me to summon it. Before this whole kingdom tears itself apart."

Just then, a soft chime sounded at the door. A royal courier entered, bowing deeply. "Your Highnesses. A message from the Crown."

Frigid took the scroll with trembling fingers. She broke the seal, her breath catching as she read.

"He's called a Parliament session. Two days from now. Full assembly."

Freija stood abruptly. "He's going to make it public."

Frigid's hand fell to her side. Her voice was hollow. "Once he speaks the decree before Parliament, it's law. There's no turning back."

Later That Night – The Terrace

The icy wind howled across the terraces behind the palace. Frigid stood near the edge, her hands resting on the frozen balustrade, staring into the falling snow. Freija approached slowly, cloaked in silence, Kimiko not far behind.

Frigid didn't look at them. "It's not just about what Father wants anymore. If the Parliament agrees, if they ratify it, then I'll have no choice. To disobey is to be exiled. Branded as a traitor to Icelandia."

"Then let them try," Freija said. "You're not going through this alone."

Frigid turned. Her eyes were red. "I don't want you to be the backup, Freija. That's what terrifies me the most. If I falter, if I run – he'll choose you. And you'll say yes just to protect me."

Freija stepped forward and pulled her sister into a hug. "Then we don't give him the chance. We find the Gatekeeper first. We find its truth – not his version of it."

Kimiko's voice was soft but resolute. "Lysari mentioned ancient markers. Runes older than the Scrolls. We may not find the Gatekeeper, but we might find where its influence touched the land. That's a start."

Frigid sniffed and wiped her eyes. "We'll need access to the old observatory vaults. The ones hidden beneath the Temple of Hollow Sky. They contain celestial maps – records of the last convergence."

Freija nodded. "Then that's where we go."

The Next Morning – Queen Glaciana's Study

Queen Glaciana stood at her desk, reading the royal summons. Her expression was unreadable.

"He moves faster than I feared," she said. "He intends to make this permanent. Official."

Freija, Kimiko, and Frigid stood before her, weary from a night with little sleep.

Frigid spoke first. "We have less than two days. That's all the time we have to find something – anything – to stop this."

The Queen turned to them, something softening in her gaze. "Then go. I will do what I can to stall him. Perhaps I can delay the session with a petition of procedural inquiry. It will raise questions, but I no longer care."

Kimiko stepped forward. "Your Majesty, if we find what we're looking for – what then?"

Glaciana's eyes flickered toward the fire. "Then we find the courage to face the truth. Whatever it may be."

Freija placed her hand on her mother's shoulder. "Thank you. For believing us."

The Queen smiled faintly. "I never stopped. I only feared the stories I once told you as children were more dangerous than comforting."

Outside, the storm clouds swirled.

Inside, a quiet rebellion began to take shape.

And the race to find the Gatekeeper had begun.

Secrets Beneath the Stone

The hidden chamber lay deep beneath the Temple of the Hollow Sky, accessible only through a narrow passageway concealed by centuries of snow-packed ice. Frigid led the way, guiding Freija and Kimiko through the winding halls beneath the old observatory vaults. The only light came from enchanted lanterns that shimmered in pale white hues, casting ghost-like shadows across the frost-streaked walls.

"This section hasn't been opened in generations," Frigid whispered, her breath visible in the frigid air. "Not even Parliament archivists know it exists."

Kimiko said nothing, her eyes scanning every surface, every marking etched into the stone. Her fingers hovered over the hilts of her katanas instinctively, though the silence down here was ancient and undisturbed.

Freija moved close to her sister. "Are you sure this is safe?"

Frigid allowed herself a tight smile. "Absolutely not."

The passage ended at a tall doorway framed in obsidian and bone-white frost. Ancient runes glowed faintly across its surface, flickering as if sensing the royal bloodline approaching. Frigid pressed her hand against the center rune, and the door hissed open, releasing a gust of stale, frozen air.

Inside was a domed chamber, circular and vast. The walls were lined with tiered alcoves, each holding scrolls wrapped in frost-silk, crystals imbued with memory spells, and tomes bound in glacierhide. The ceiling was adorned with a mural of Icelandia's four continents encircling a central winged figure cloaked in radiance.

Freija stared up. "The Gatekeeper."

Frigid nodded solemnly. "This chamber is older than the palace itself. It was built in the era after the wars between the continents, when the first unification treaties were signed."

Kimiko walked the perimeter, her fingers trailing near the stone. "The mural shows the elementals too. One for each continent. They're bound to the land."

Frigid pulled a crystal tome from a recess and set it on a pedestal in the center of the room. "We may not be able to stop Father. But if we can learn how the Gatekeeper was once invoked, maybe we can do it without sacrificing anyone."

The three women worked in silence for over an hour. The air in the chamber grew colder as they unearthed scrolls depicting ancient rituals, celestial alignments, and bloodline seals. Several texts referenced the elemental prisons sealed beneath each continent – and how royal families once acted as guardians to these sites.

"This scroll mentions a ritual of communion," Freija said, unfurling a sheet lined with interwoven script and illustrations. "Royal blood was needed to activate these protections. But it doesn't give the specifics."

Frigid nodded. "That's been the theme in everything I've found so far. General descriptions. Symbolic references. But never the full rite."

Kimiko remained quiet, focused on a fragmented scroll written in the oldest Icelandia dialect. Her gaze lingered on a phrase repeated several times near an emblem of the Gatekeeper – a silhouette bathed in light, bound by five threads.

"'Heart must guide the pact,'" Kimiko read aloud. "'Royal blood, willingly given, opens the Vessel. The guardian awakens only through harmony.'"

Frigid turned to her. "That confirms what Lysari said. But we're still missing the actual process. The incantation. The offering. The bond."

Freija frowned. "Could it be encoded? Hidden somewhere else in this archive?"

Frigid shook her head. "No. It's missing. Look here – this index crystal references two separate scrolls specifically focused on the Binding of the Fifth Light. The Gatekeeper. But the alcoves where they should be... they're empty."

Freija walked to the slots and peered into the gaps. Dust lined the interiors, undisturbed for centuries. "They weren't moved recently. They've been gone for years."

"Stolen?" Kimiko asked.

"Or lost to time," Frigid murmured. "If they were taken during the last uprising, they may have been destroyed or hidden to protect them. Or perhaps Father has them."

Freija's fists clenched. "That would explain why he thinks he knows how to use the ritual. But if he's working from fragments, or only half the truth..."

"He could be invoking something dangerous," Kimiko finished. "Worse – he might not actually summon the Gatekeeper at all."

They stood in silence, the flickering lanterns casting long shadows behind them.

Frigid ran a hand over the pedestal's surface. "If we can't find the scrolls... we'll have to find the Gatekeeper ourselves. And hope it speaks."

Freija met her eyes. "Then we start at the convergence. Wherever the mural leads. We follow it."

Kimiko gave a small nod. Her face was unreadable, but her hand lingered at her Frostheart charm longer than usual.

Unspoken thoughts drifted among them, heavy as the frost-laced air. The Gatekeeper might yet be their only hope – but without the ritual, without understanding, it remained just as mysterious – and just as dangerous – as the very forces they sought to stop.

As they gathered what scrolls they could carry, Freija paused beneath the mural one last time. The figure at the center – wreathed in light, arms and wings extended – seemed almost to watch them.

Whatever path lay ahead, they would walk it soon.

Together.

The Night Before

Stacks of scrolls lay scattered across every available surface of Frigid's private chambers. The crystal-topped tables were covered in old parchment, memory-etched tablets, and frost-lined tomes. Flickering ice lanterns hung overhead, casting a pale glow over the endless script – runes of old Icelandian history, prophecy, and myth.

Freija sat slumped in a high-backed chair, chin resting in her hand as she stared down at the open text in front of her. Her short white hair had fallen over her eyes, and her frost-blue wings were slouched low in fatigue, tips twitching faintly with restless tension.

"This one only reiterates what we already know," she muttered. "Royal blood, harmony, the fifth light. It's all repetition. Nothing new."

Kimiko crouched by a smaller table in the corner, scanning a carved obsidian tablet through a spectral lens. Her movements were meticulous, eyes sharp, but even her usually quiet confidence had frayed at the edges. "These symbols... their meaning is unchanged from the Vault's riddles. The same words, same mythic references. But no instructions. Nothing that helps us stand against tomorrow."

Frigid stood rigid at the center of the room, pacing, her double-ended spear propped nearby. Her silver wings, usually precise and poised, shifted tightly behind her back with every turn. She held a crumbling scroll, half-translated. Her voice came out measured and cold but with a tremor below the surface, "I spent half my life preparing for this: balancing elements, memorizing scrolls, weaving magic through Parliament. They taught me about the power regime of this world. But tonight... tonight we realize those lessons may have been lies."

She stopped by the hearth, staring into the soft red-yellow flame. "The ritual was lost or taken. And without it... there's no safe way to summon the Gatekeeper."

Kimiko stood and crossed her arms. "And if we guess wrong, we risk invoking the wrong entity entirely. The Gatekeeper isn't the only force that responds to royal blood on this world."

"Or sacrifice," Freija added bitterly.

Silence settled over the room.

Freija looked up, eyes hollowed by sleepless nights, hair spiked and frozen at the tips. The Frostheart charm at her neck pulsed faintly, a quiet rhythm echoing her anxiety. Her wings shivered slightly, feathers ruffling as if responding to the turmoil within. "Parliament meets at dawn. They've already heard Father's word. If they agree, one of us will be bound."

Freija gaze flicked to Frigid. Worry overwhelmed her tired face. "If you refuse, they'll choose me. If I refuse, they'll find someone else. Maybe even Mother. It's... it's inevitable. If it comes to Mother, you know she will do it."

The silence that followed felt too big to occupy. Kimiko stood, drawing in a deliberate breath that seemed to still time. She looked back and forth at the two sisters, "This isn't logic. It's not prophecy... it's desperation. Wrong person, wrong ceremony... and we risk conjuring something worse than an elemental."

Freija's humor cut through her despair like ice, "Or we invite it for tea and hand it the keys to the kingdom... our kingdom."

Frigid's face flickered with anger and sorrow as she dropped onto the bench. She stared into the lantern flame as though it held every answer. Her wings slowly folded around her like a cocoon. "They call me Princess Frigid... cool, disciplined, loyal. But tomorrow... tomorrow they will call me Gatekeeper's Vessel. And I won't be ready."

Lucidity flashed through Freija's eyes, painfully shared. "I thought they told me I was strong... but not this strong."

Kimiko placed a steady hand on Frigid's arm. Her voice was calm but resolute, "Then we hold something stronger. Tonight, we stay together."

Frigid's eyes glistened... even in the forgiving glow of ice lanterns.

The three women stood close. Freija's frost-dusted wings lightly brushed against Frigid's cloak; Kimiko's katana shimmered in its sheath at her side. Despite the silence, a bond pulsed warmer than any fire.

Freija said with a resounding sigh, "We still have tonight. A single sliver of time to find a path away from dread."

Frigid closed her eyes, swallowing grief and frustration, "I'm tired of being the dutiful one. Tonight... I want to fight for myself... for us."

Kimiko shook her head, whispering almost to herself, "Then we go deeper... through knowledge, not power. Through choice, not blood."

Freija finished softly, "Into heart."

The three nodded together, unspoken understanding flowing between them.

They shuffled through the scrolls, determined to comb every line, decipher every half-remembered rhyme. The hourglass ran low. Shadows shifted behind their eyes, not from the flickering lanterns, but from depths unearthed within.

After hours had passed, snow began to swirl outside, pressing against frostglass windows like a silent witness. The palace seemed asleep; only the ice whispered beneath the moonlight. Inside, the sisters and Kimiko burnished the final fragments of prophecy.

Freija closed her eyes, running her fingers through her short white hair, her wings drooping slightly with exhaustion. "May the Gatekeeper... or whoever answers... hear the truth in midnight's words... and find mercy in our hearts."

Frigid folded the last tablet with care. Her wings now hung quietly behind her, burdened but no longer clenched. "We may step into tomorrow battered, but... not broken. We will be more than their choices."

Kimiko slid the lens back into her sash pocket, "This room... this night... it's our silent vow. Whatever dawn brings, we stand in the quiet between us. That no matter who tries to bind either of you... we decide."

They released each other's hands in a final gesture of unity. Freija brushed a snowflake from Frigid's shoulder; Kimiko clasped them both silently.

Footsteps outside murmured. Their shadowed forms slipped into place... prepared, though terrified. The door closed behind them with a crisp click.

The ice-lanterns followed their silhouettes into darkness, as the snowstorms roared and dawn crept closer, bringing with it law, ritual, choice... and perhaps, sacrifice.

But in that moment of twilight, sorrows, and doubling fears, the three women held something stronger than power: their shared resolve.

The hour crept past midnight. Snow continued to fall, masking their tracks. Though no words followed them, each knew one thing: time was no longer on their side. Tomorrow, everything will change. But tonight... tonight, they held the cold and each other close.

Before the Judgment

The Queen's Chambers

The snow outside the royal palace had thickened, blanketing Frostholm in quiet stillness. But within the Queen's private chambers, tension thundered like a blizzard.

"Frostran, please... don't do this." Glaciana's voice cracked as she took hold of the King's sleeve. "She's your daughter."

The King stood before the frostglass window, his gaze locked on the distant spires of the Parliament Hall. He wore his ceremonial robes – dark, regal, trimmed in the ancient sigils of his bloodline. There was resolve in his eyes, colder than any winter wind.

"She is also the future of our people," he said, not turning. "If she must carry the burden, it will be with honor."

Glaciana moved to stand beside him. "It's not her burden, Frostran. It's yours. Yours to carry, yours to fix. But you've passed it to her – on the thinnest understanding of a myth."

"The Gatekeeper is not a myth," Frostran replied. "You've seen the signs. The world fractures more each day. Storms, tremors, fire, collapse... the seals are weakening. We either awaken the Gatekeeper or face elemental ruin."

"And at what cost?" she whispered her hands trembling as she grips her sleeve. Her wings fully flaring in desperation as if she just wanted to fly away.

He finally turned to her, his voice heavy. "Would you have me let the world die to spare one life?"

She stared at him for a long moment. "Yes," she said. "If that life is our daughter."

The King's jaw tightened. "Then you no longer understand the weight of the crown."

Glaciana stepped back as if struck. Her voice lowered to a whisper. "And you no longer understand the meaning of love."

He didn't respond.

When he left the room moments later, the frost on the windows bloomed into spiderwebs of ice.

In Frigid's Chambers

In her chambers, Frigid stood in silence before a full-length mirror carved from polished glacier stone. She was already in her formal Parliament robes – deep navy with silver stitching and a platinum shoulder clasp bearing her family's crest. Her hands trembled as she adjusted her sash.

Freija stood behind her, arms crossed, worry etched into every line of her face.

"You don't have to do this," Freija said softly.

Frigid's reflection didn't flinch. "He's the King. I'm a Parliament representative. My loyalty is to the realm."

"To the realm, yes. But to him?" Freija's voice was sharper now. "He's using you, Frigid. You know that."

Frigid turned slowly, the tension in her shoulders finally cracking. "What would you have me do, Freija? Defy him? Disgrace our name? Be stripped of my title? Be exiled?"

Freija stepped forward, grabbing her sister's hands. "I'd have you live. I'd have you be free to choose your fate, not have it carved into your skin by ancient law."

Tears welled in Frigid's eyes, but she blinked them away. "I am afraid," she admitted. "I dream of drowning in ice. Of being hollowed out."

Freija pulled her into an embrace, her voice thick. "Then run. With me. With Kimiko. We'll find another way."

But Frigid didn't return the hug. Her voice came as a whisper. "If I run… you'll be chosen instead."

Freija froze.

"You have the blood," Frigid continued. "And the heart of a protector. If I refuse, they'll look to you. And I won't survive watching them tear you apart for their savior."

Freija stepped back, breath caught in her throat.

Frigid adjusted her robes once more. "I have to do this."

A Gift from the Queen

A soft knock came at the door. A palace messenger bowed low. "Princess Frigid... Her Majesty asks for your presence. Alone."

Frigid exchanged a final glance with Freija, then followed the attendant through the silent corridors of the palace. The castle walls hummed with chill, the frostglass glowing with threads of blue.

Inside the Queen's private solar, Glaciana stood near a round basin of shimmering water. She turned when Frigid entered, her face drawn but warm.

"I asked you here," the Queen said, "not as sovereign... but as your mother."

Frigid bowed her head, unsure of how to speak.

Glaciana crossed the room slowly and took her daughter's hands. "You've always been my still one. My steady snow. You didn't need warnings like Freija, or fire-forged instincts like Kimiko. You lived here... inside the palace... within protections I thought would never be tested."

She reached into a small box atop her writing desk and withdrew a delicate necklace. The charm was crystal, shaped like a teardrop encasing a pulsing violet glow. Its edges flickered with a faint, almost imperceptible trace of energy.

"This is a Frostheart," Glaciana said, fastening it around Frigid's neck with trembling fingers. "But not like the ones your sister or Kimiko wear. This one was made... for you. It warns of danger, yes... but it also reflects the wearer's inner strength. And when the moment comes, it amplifies that strength in return."

Frigid touched the pendant, her hands shaking. "I never thought I'd need one."

"I never thought I'd send you to face what lies ahead," Glaciana whispered, her voice cracking. "But if I can't protect you... then let this remind you that someone always loves you, beyond the weight of crown or ceremony."

Frigid's breath hitched as her mother pulled her into a fierce, tender embrace. Their wings folded into each other instinctively, Glaciana's sweeping and elegant, Frigid's slightly trembling but held firm. They clung there in the hush, a private farewell spoken only in heartbeats.

When they parted, Glaciana cupped her daughter's face gently. "Come back to me. Whatever happens... come back."

Frigid nodded, unable to speak. She turned slowly and left the chamber, her wings tightening slightly against her back. The violet charm pulsed softly against her chest as she stepped into the corridors, the weight of both legacy and love guiding her steps.

At Parliament's Doors

Two hours later, the Parliament Hall opened its heavy rune-carved doors.

Dignitaries from all four continents entered in procession – each dressed in their regional attire, bearing emblems of their cities and powers. Murmurs filled the great domed chamber as boots clicked against polished crystal floors and wings shifted around ceremonial cloaks.

Frigid entered through the side reserved for Parliament members. Her face was composed, masklike. She took her seat near the front of the chamber, her gaze fixed forward. Her wings bore a weight that showed her dread, and the violet Frostheart charm around her neck pulsed faintly with each breath.

From her tiered seat in the royal court, Freija's eyes locked onto the unfamiliar glow. Her brows furrowed slightly.

"She's wearing a Frostheart," she whispered to her mother.

Glaciana nodded, her voice barely audible. "I gave it to her this morning. A special one... crafted with memory stone and violet flame. It resonates with her inner strength."

Freija's throat tightened. "She's never needed one before."

"She does now," the Queen replied, gaze never leaving her daughter. "And she knows it."

Kimiko entered last, guided by a palace attendant. She wore her black battle gi, formalized only slightly by a white ceremonial sash. She was seated in the section reserved for foreign dignitaries and honored

82

guests. Her sharp eyes also found the violet charm, and though she said nothing, her hand brushed instinctively over her own.

All three women sat in different parts of the hall. All three locked eyes across the vast chamber. Then the great bell tolled once. Parliament was called to order.

The King's Decree

The Parliament Hall shimmered beneath the light of crystal orbs that floated high above the chamber. Rows of dignitaries, emissaries, and royal officials from all four continents sat in perfect formation, their expressions ranging from curious to grim. A hush fell over the room as the King of Icelandia, Frostran, stepped forward onto the elevated dais.

He wore a mantle of glacial velvet trimmed with ancient runes, and his presence alone commanded attention. With a wave of his hand, the floor beneath the dais flared softly – activating a projection of Icelandia's four continents across the ice-floor.

He raised his voice – not in anger, but with the cadence of command.

"Honored representatives of the Northern, Southern, Eastern, and Western continents… I have summoned you here not for ceremony, but for survival."

He gestured toward the flickering map.

"Our world bleeds beneath our feet. You've heard the rumors. Let me now speak plainly."

He extended his hand, and one quadrant of the map expanded, illuminating the jagged fire-scarred cliffs of Skarae the Eastern Continent. "Wildfires consuming towns at impossible speed. Firestorms that resist frostcraft. Entire regions abandoned."

He moved to another quadrant – depicting the storm-battered islands of Dorland the Southern Continent. "Windstorms that tear through our trade fleets. Hurricanes appearing without warning. The air itself has turned against us."

The next image revealed the mountains of Sommara the Western Continent. "Quakes and sinkholes have collapsed villages. Entire valleys swallowed whole. The land is cracking – fracturing as though it seeks to awaken."

Finally, he displayed Icecrest the Northern Continent. "And here, in our heartland, ice slides consume outposts. Glaciers shift without cause. The Vault beneath Mount Solance trembles, and the Harbinger stirs."

Murmurs spread through the chamber. Some looked shaken. Others are skeptical. Frigid's eyes moved across the crowd, reading their faces – some pale with fear, others drawn tight with disbelief. A few looked to her already, as if bracing for the King's inevitable direction.

Frostran raised his voice.

"These are not natural disasters. These are the symptoms of a larger truth. The ancient elementals, once subdued by our ancestors, are awakening. One from each continent. Fire, wind, stone… and ice."

Kimiko leaned forward slightly in her seat. Her eyes were locked on Frostran, her hand unconsciously brushing the Frostheart charm at her neck. She could see that Freija's fists were balled tightly in her lap, her jaw clenched as she sat on the edge of her seat.

He let the silence settle before continuing.

"Long ago, in the darkest chapter of our world's history, four elemental forces waged war upon this planet. They were stopped not by armies – but by the intervention of a fifth being. The Gatekeeper. A force of balance. Of order. Of heart."

He raised a hand, and two scrolls floated forward into the light, bound in shimmering frostlace.

"These scrolls are ancient – preserved in our royal vaults, translated by the finest scholars and truth-seers. They speak of the Gatekeeper's bond. A ritual of fusion. The Gatekeeper cannot exist in this realm unaided. It must anchor itself in a body of royal blood. A person whose heart is pure and loyal to the people. This is the Vessel."

Freija's heart sank. She felt it – the slow, inevitable dread creeping down her spine.

"This is not a legend," Frostran declared. "It is history… It is prophecy… It is law."

He turned, locking eyes with Frigid across the chamber. Her breath caught in her throat. *He couldn't mean…*

"The Vessel… shall be my eldest daughter. Parliament member Frigid of the royal house. Her discipline, her duty, her devotion to

Icelandia proves her worth. And her royal blood binds her to the Gatekeeper's legacy."

A collective gasp rippled through the chamber. Frigid's heart thundered in her chest. Her wings began to flutter noticeably. She looked around quickly – at the stunned faces of her fellow Parliament members. A few nodded in grave agreement. Others averted their eyes. None stood in protest.

On the other side of the room, Queen Glaciana's hand rose to her mouth, her composure cracking. Freija's eyes blazed, but she said nothing – protocol kept her still.

Kimiko's gaze turned sharply toward Frigid, her expression unreadable.

"I call upon this Parliament," Frostran continued, "to approve the ritual by a two-thirds vote, as prescribed by Article 11 of the High Accord. Let our voices declare the path forward."

Frigid felt numb. Her mind reeled, but her body moved automatically as the vote was called. One by one, members stood and cast their vote.

"Aye."

"Aye."

"Aye."

Each word echoed like a dagger in Frigid's chest. And still – she stood. *I can't believe I am about to seal my own fate,* she thought.

Frigid looked down at the purple Frostheart around her neck. She placed two fingers on it. Turning to face Freija, "Aye."

Freija's breath caught with tears running down her face. She watched in disbelief as her sister, stoic and regal, joined the majority sealing her own fate.

Only one dissenting vote was registered – from a representative of Sommara. He looked deeply unsettled but bowed to the majority.

The King nodded solemnly.

"Then it is law."

He looked toward the Parliament.

"We will adjourn for two hours to allow for preparations. The ritual site – an ancient chamber located beneath the Icespire Sanctuary – will be opened. Only key officials and members of the royal family may attend."

His voice rang with finality.

"Dismissed."

The crystal bell rang again.

And the Parliament began to empty.

Queen Glaciana remained seated, her shoulders rigid, wings half unfurled beating like a heartbeat, eyes filled with tears that refused to fall.

Freija sat frozen, her body thrumming with suppressed rage. Kimiko stood slowly, watching Frigid with intensity and a couple of tears coming from her eyes.

Frigid remained upright, unmoving. She had voted for her own fate – and now, she would be led to it.

The echo of footsteps across the frostglass floor was the only sound.

Outside the palace, snow began to fall again, slow and silent.

As if the planet itself was mourning. Or bracing.

The Binding of the Gatekeeper

The Summit of Ritual

The bonding chamber was a relic of another age, hidden deep beneath the palace in the oldest sections of the Icevault – far older than even the Parliament's secret archives. Hewn from the mountain itself, it stretched out as a massive open space carved into an ancient glacial ravine. A broad stone balcony jutted over a yawning pit that extended deep into the mountain's heart. From this balcony extended a circular platform suspended by arcane pillars of ice and crystal, glowing faintly in anticipation of ancient rites being rekindled.

Frigid stood upon the balcony dressed in ceremonial white robes that shimmered like woven frost. She was still wearing the Frostheart charm around her neck that her mother gave to her earlier.

Frigid's long hair had been braided and pinned with silver fastenings shaped like snowflakes and icicles, but her regal composure was cracking. The closer the moment came, the more her pale hands trembled.

On either side of the balcony, King Frostran and Queen Glaciana stood dressed in their formal regalia. The King looked proud – resolute – but his eyes betrayed the burden of sacrifice. The Queen's hands were clenched tightly, white-knuckled, though her face remained solemn. Nearby stood Freija, armored but quiet, her fists clenched at her sides. Kimiko, silent and unreadable, lingered a step behind, the Frostheart charms at lady's neck pulsing like a warning beacon in unison.

A handful of Parliament members watched from a raised overlook to the side, flanked by royal guards. Two elderly mages in robes so old they seemed woven from the past itself stood at the edge of the platform, each holding one of the ancient scrolls. Their voices echoed as they spoke in tandem.

"To awaken the Guardian of Balance, the one known as the Gatekeeper, a Vessel must be chosen – one of royal blood, of unwavering loyalty, and of a heart forged in duty."

The words hung heavy in the chamber. Freija stepped forward and pulled Frigid into a fierce embrace. Freija wings were half fully unfurled, trembling.

"You don't have to do this," she whispered.

Frigid's breath shook. "I do. It's my duty."

Their embrace lingered, a rare show of vulnerability between the twin sisters who had grown up mirroring each other's strengths but diverging in their hearts. Freija stepped back, her eyes shining with unshed tears. The King approached next, placing a firm hand on Frigid's shoulder.

"You are stronger than you believe," he said. "Today, you protect all of Icelandia."

Frigid nodded, but her gaze flickered to the vast chasm below. Her mouth twitched – not in resolve, but fear.

The Queen embraced her last. For once, the steel in Glaciana's posture melted away. "Come back to me, daughter," she whispered.

Frigid stepped onto the platform, alone.

The mages raised their scrolls. Ancient runes flared across the chamber walls in spectral blue, casting the scene in an ethereal glow. Wind began to spiral up from the pit, curling around the platform, lifting ice particles into a vortex of swirling energy.

The Frostheart charm on Frigid's chest throbbed wildly. A circular glyph beneath her feet ignited with blue light, and from the void below, something emerged – a mist, shimmering with blue-white essence, coalescing into a formless spirit. It hovered, pulsing like a heartbeat of the world.

Frigid lifted her head, eyes wide. The mist surged toward her.

Then came the heart shattering scream.

Frigid's body arched backward, her arms flailing as energy wrapped around her like chains. Her wings snapped fully open, trying to take flight but instead spasming under the strain. The blue mist crackled with chaotic energy, as if the ritual had spiraled out of control.

"She's in pain!" Queen Glaciana cried.

"Hold the bond!" one of the mages shouted.

Freija lunged forward. "You're killing her!"

King Frostran raised a hand, stunned. *This wasn't what was supposed to happen like this.*

Frigid collapsed to her knees, screaming again as tendrils of the Gatekeeper's spirit attempted to bore into her chest. Her charm faded to nothingness.

Freija didn't wait. She dashed forward.

But Kimiko was faster.

Without a word, the ninja vaulted over the railing and landed on the platform, reaching Frigid and hauling her backward, out of the summoning glyph. The moment Frigid left the circle, the spirit stopped – hovering midair, humming with raw energy, now detached and pulsing.

Kimiko knelt, holding Frigid, who gasped and clutched at her side.

"It didn't accept me," Frigid said weakly, eyes wide with terror. "It rejected me."

Freija reached the platform moments later and dropped beside them. "You're okay now. It's over."

But it wasn't. The blue-white mist remained, waiting.

Then the Frostheart charm around Kimiko's neck began to pulse erratically, almost violently. Since Kimiko's back was to the group only her eyes and Frigid could see this happen.

Kimiko's hand rose to her chest, gripping the charm. Her breath taught.

It was calling to her.

She looked at Freija, then at the King. Her expression, as always, was unreadable – until she stood.

Kimiko turned toward Frostran, her voice cutting through the magical winds. "I am of royal blood. My father was a samurai lord. My ancestors ruled over their clan with honor. I am his daughter. His legacy. I am royal."

The King's eyes narrowed. "You are not of Icelandia."

Kimiko stepped forward, each word measured and resolute. "The scrolls speak of royal blood. They do not specify from where it must come."

The Queen took a sharp breath. Freija stood, eyes wide, heart pounding.

"Let me do this," Kimiko said. "You need a Vessel of heart. Of loyalty. Of blood. I am all three. I've fought to protect this world, though it's not mine. And I will not let my friends suffer."

The King hesitated. "This cannot be…"

Kimiko moved before he could object. She stepped into the summoning circle. The mist pulsed as if it recognized her presence.

"Kimiko, NO!" Freija cried, stepping forward.

Kimiko turned her head slightly and, for once, smiled. "Relax, Freija. I'll be okay."

The mages raised their scrolls once more. Ancient symbols lit the air as the ritual reignited.

The spirit surged toward Kimiko, this time not as an attack, but an embrace. Energy wrapped around her form like a cloak, wind spiraling upward as the platform shook.

Kimiko threw her head back and screamed as the Gatekeeper poured into her. Her body arched, glowing with blinding light. Her Frostheart charm began to glow as bright as a star.

Her eyes snapped open.

They were no longer black.

They were glowing blue-white. Luminous. Infinite.

The aura around her shimmered like a lightning storm – tendrils of frost and energy swirling in tandem.

Kimiko stood at the center of it all, calm now, arms lowered. Her expression was unreadable. Ethereal.

When she spoke, her voice echoed – not just as herself, but layered, as if another being spoke with her.

"I am bound. I awakened. I see through new eyes."

The mages fell to their knees in awe.

Freija stepped forward, heart thundering. "Kimiko!?!"

She turned her glowing gaze to her friend. The voice softened. "I'm here."

Freija's legs gave out, and she sank to her knees, overcome by emotion.

Behind her, the King stared in awe.

The Queen turned away, tears finally spilling.

Frigid, still trembling, whispered, "You saved me."

And far above them, as if the mountain itself had heard the spirit's rebirth, the wind stilled.

But far beneath the ice, the other forces stirred.
The Gatekeeper had now returned from his slumber.

The Spirit Within

The King's private chambers had never felt more sacred, or more uncertain. The fire in the hearth glowed with a steady reddish hue, casting icy shadows against the crystalline walls. Thick tapestries dampened the chill, though no amount of insulation could shield the room from the weight that now pressed in on everyone gathered.

Seated at the great obsidian table, King Frostran rested his arms across a spread of newly unfurled scrolls. His composure was firm, but for the first time in recent memory, his face showed the furrowed creases of a ruler who had been wrong. The Queen sat beside him, her hands folded tightly in her lap, a fine tremble in her fingers. Her wings were slightly opening and closing mimicking her long breaths.

Across from them, the two ancient mages stood with scrolls still clutched to their chests, their expressions unreadable, as if waiting to be summoned into counsel. To the side sat Frigid and Freija, both still in their ceremonial robes, their eyes betraying exhaustion and fraying emotions.

Kimiko stood alone, her arms crossed tightly over her chest. The aura of the Gatekeeper still clung to her, visible even now in the faint flickers of blue-white light that shimmered around her shoulders. Her eyes, no longer black but glowing with that impossible celestial blue, scanned the faces before her.

It was the Queen who spoke first. "How do we begin to explain this?"

No one answered.

Kimiko finally stepped forward. Her voice, though still hers, carried a subtle echo. "By accepting what is. Not what was expected."

The King sat back. "You weren't meant to be the Vessel. The Gatekeeper was destined for someone of Icelandian royal blood. For my daughter."

Frigid, sitting still and pale, winced at the reminder. Her wings almost betraying the emotions she felt.

Kimiko looked over to Frigid. "It rejected her not because she lacked strength or loyalty. She has both in abundance."

One of the mages cleared his throat. "The Vessel must be royal. Of unbroken bloodlines. But more than that, the Vessel must be of purpose – of heart and selfless spirit. We assumed those traits would be bound to the same blood. Perhaps we assumed wrong."

Freija interjected, her voice rough with emotion. "You knew this could happen?"

The other mage bowed his head. "We knew... that the Gatekeeper's choice might not align with our designations. It is a force of balance. It chooses not by lineage alone, but by something deeper. Something ancient."

Kimiko stepped further into the center of the room. "I did not expect to be chosen. But it recognized my intent. My willingness to protect."

Frigid looked down. "But I would have protected Icelandia. I was willing."

"You were," Kimiko and the Gatekeeper said gently speaking in unison. "But that willingness was twisted by fear. Not fear of death – you were brave. But fear of disobedience. Of betraying duty. You feared failing your kingdom more than you feared for yourself. The Gatekeeper saw that."

The Queen finally looked up. "And in you, it saw something else?"

Kimiko hesitated, then nodded. "In me, it saw one who has no throne to return to. No legacy to uphold. Only a promise to stand between danger and those I care for. That, perhaps, was what it needed most."

Freija wiped her eyes. "I hate this. I hate that Frigid nearly died. I hate that you had to go through this, Kimiko. But damn it..." She looked up. "Thank you." Another tear appeared in one of her eyes.

Kimiko offered a warm and loving smile, tilting her head to one side.

Frostran leaned forward. "So, what now? What do you feel, Gatekeeper?"

Kimiko blinked, and when she spoke again, the echo in her voice remained. "There is much still sleeping beneath the ice. I am not whole.

My memories are scattered – but I know the others stir. The elementals. They test the bonds that kept them imprisoned. One by one, they will rise. That day will be any time now."

One of the mages stepped forward. "Then we must act. We must prepare."

The King nodded slowly, eyes locked on Kimiko. "You are the Vessel now. You carry a power older than our bloodlines. Whatever doubts I had, I set them aside. Guide us, Gatekeeper. Where do we begin?"

Kimiko turned to the frostglass window. Snow drifted gently on the wind beyond.

"We begin by listening. By watching the signs. And when the next seal weakens..."

She turned back to face them.

"...We move before the elementals do."

And though she stood still, the presence within her seemed to shimmer like a storm ready to awaken.

A Flicker of Power

The return to Frigid's chambers was quiet – eerily so. After the breathtaking and terrifying events in the binding chamber, the three women moved without speaking, their steps synchronized more from shared exhaustion than intent. Frigid led the way through the empty palace halls, her robe still draped over her shoulders, trailing with a regal hush. Freija stayed close to Kimiko, who walked with a stiff grace, the blue-white glow still faintly radiating from her skin.

As the door to Frigid's chambers sealed behind them, the silence snapped.

Freija immediately turned to Kimiko. "Are you okay?"

Kimiko sat down slowly on the edge of the crystalline bench near the hearth, her breath finally catching. The soft aura of the Gatekeeper's energy was fading, though her Frostheart pendant still shimmered faintly against her chest.

"I don't know," she said honestly still speaking in unison.

Frigid stepped closer, crouching in front of her. "You were glowing. More so than now. And, your eyes – your entire body. It was like something ancient took hold of you. Is it... is it still there?"

Kimiko hesitated and then smiled. Then she nodded.

"Yes. It's still inside me. But it doesn't speak like a voice. It's more like... a feeling. A presence. Sometimes I sense it observing. Sometimes it presses forward, as if trying to show me something. But it hasn't taken over. Not yet."

Freija sat beside her. "Do you feel in control?"

Kimiko looked down at her hands, watching the faint shimmer of blue run across her skin before fading. "Mostly. But there are moments – brief flashes – when I feel like I could level a mountain if I wasn't careful."

Frigid exchanged a glance with her sister. "Can you communicate with it? Ask it questions?"

"I've tried," Kimiko said. "When I'm calm, I can sense thoughts. Impressions. Feelings. But not words. Not yet. It's like it's... waiting."

Freija leaned forward. "Waiting for what?"

Kimiko shook her head slowly. "I don't know. Maybe for the elementals to rise. Maybe for me to be ready. It's like the Gatekeeper isn't entirely sure I can handle it yet."

Frigid frowned, her brow furrowed in thought. "It didn't accept me. But it accepted you instantly. Do you think it chose you because of your bloodline? Or something else?"

Kimiko closed her eyes. "Maybe both. My father taught me honor, duty, loyalty. The life of the samurai isn't about power – it's about service. Maybe the Gatekeeper sensed that. That I'm willing to protect rather than command."

Freija smiled softly. "You've always been like that. Even when we fought side-by-side during the Necra War. You never boasted. Never hesitated to throw yourself between danger and your team."

Kimiko exhaled a short laugh. "Some would call that recklessness."

"Some would call that loyalty," Frigid said quietly.

The three sat in stillness for a moment, the fire casting shadows against the walls of the icy chamber.

"There's something else," Kimiko admitted. "I can feel... empathy. Like the Gatekeeper is filtering my emotions – heightening them. It's making me more aware of what people feel. I could sense your pain, Frigid, when the bond rejected you. It hit me like a blade. And Freija – your fear when you thought you might lose her. That overwhelmed me."

Freija blinked. "You felt that?"

"Like it was my own."

Frigid leaned back slightly, stunned. "So this bond... it's not just power. It's emotional."

Kimiko nodded. "Yes. It's changing me. I've spent my life controlling my emotions, keeping them locked away. Now, I don't think I can anymore."

Freija touched her shoulder gently. "That's not a weakness, Kimiko. That's your strength now."

For a long moment, Kimiko just breathed. Then, with a slow exhale, she said the words that surprised even her, "I'm scared."

Frigid reached for her hand. "We're with you. Every step of this."

Kimiko gave her a grateful nod and a faint smile. "Thank you. Both of you. I don't know what's coming. But I know I don't want to face it alone."

Freija smiled, and for once, there was no teasing in her voice. Only sincerity. "Then you won't."

The Frostheart pendants of all three women pulsed in unison – soft, warm, and steady.

Outside, the night winds howled through the palace corridors.

But inside that chamber, a bond of trust had been reforged.

Mapping the Threat

Frigid paced the length of her frostlit chamber, the soft glow of enchanted runes trailing beneath her footsteps. Snow drifted lazily beyond the high windows, blanketing the spires of Frostholm in muted silence. A fire crackled in the corner, but even its warmth couldn't chase the chill tightening in the room.

Kimiko sat on the edge of the long stone bench, arms resting on her knees, her gaze steady but distant. The Frostheart charm still glowed faintly at her chest, now subtly entwined with fine threads of silvery energy – a lingering echo of the Gatekeeper's essence.

Freija leaned beside the hearth, arms folded, her eyes darting between her sister and their quiet friend. "Are you still feeling it? The pulses?"

Kimiko nodded. "They come and go. Like a heartbeat that isn't mine. It doesn't speak in words... not yet. But I sense its awareness. Its intent."

"And that intent?" Frigid asked, her voice low.

Kimiko closed her eyes. "Balance. It wants balance. But it's also searching. It doesn't know what changed while it slept. It feels... fragmented."

A knock sounded at the door. Frigid moved swiftly to open it. A palace courier stood outside, breathless and flushed from the cold. He bowed and handed her a sealed crystal scroll.

Frigid unrolled it and skimmed the contents. Her expression darkened. "It's from the Queen. The first emissaries from the other continents have arrived. Representatives from the Southern Confederation, the Western Tribes, and the Eastern Dominion. They're here for a council meeting... and they want answers."

"Then we give them answers," Freija said, stepping forward.

Meeting the Council Members

The sky over Icecrest was steel-gray, casting a muted pallor over the palace spires. Inside the Grand Strategy Hall, the temperature held a ceremonial chill, as if the room itself wished to remain impartial. Yet nothing about this meeting would be neutral.

Kimiko stood near one of the frostglass windows, her cloak drawn tight around her frame, not for warmth, but to anchor herself. Her Frostheart pendant pulsed gently against her chest, a quiet heartbeat in the silence. Though the Gatekeeper's glow was subdued, its presence remained... a storm at rest beneath her skin.

Frigid moved with deliberate poise as she set crystal tablets onto the command table, each displaying seismic activity, weather anomalies, and arcane disturbances across Icelandia. Her every motion was precise, even elegant, but her eyes betrayed the exhaustion beneath her surface. She hadn't slept since the ritual.

Freija entered last, armored and alert, her hand resting lightly on the hilt of one of her blades. She looked more like a guardian than a diplomat – eyes sharp, jaw set – but there was tension in her wings, a hesitance in how she moved. Her gaze lingered on Kimiko longer than she intended.

"The others will arrive soon," Frigid announced, voice even. "Representatives from the Southern Confederation, the Eastern Dominion, and the Western Tribes. They're here to confirm what they already fear."

Kimiko didn't turn. "And to see what I've become."

Freija stepped beside her. "Can you blame them?"

"No," Kimiko replied, her voice low. "I'd want to see me too."

The three waited in silence until the distant hum of approaching dignitaries echoed beyond the chamber doors. When they opened, the Queen and King entered first, flanked by Icelandian guards. Behind them came the foreign envoys, each representing a power whose stability had already begun to crack.

Queen Glaciana welcomed them with regal warmth, but her tone brooked no ceremony. "This is no longer about borders. The world is stirring. We must plan a coordinated response."

As she spoke, Frigid activated the central holomap. Floating above the table, the contours of Icelandia shimmered with updated readings... flashes of red and gold where the anomalies were strongest.

The Eastern envoy, Virelle, narrowed her eyes. "Skarae burns. We know that much. What we don't know is how to fight what we can't see."

Maelor of the Western Tribes crossed his arms. "And we're to believe that one warrior – foreign and fused with a forgotten being – is our solution?"

Kimiko stepped forward, eyes glowing faintly. The room dimmed as if responding to her.

"I'm not your solution. I'm part of the fight. But if we don't face this together, your tribes, your dominions, your confederations... none of them will survive."

Her words weren't dramatic. They were factual. Even Maelor, skeptical and stern, said nothing more.

Frigid turned to the group. "We'll begin the journey east in two days. We'll start at Skarae."

The Queen nodded once. "This meeting is not for promises, but awareness. You've now seen what we face. If you have agents, send them. If you have doubts, bury them. Icelandia will act."

As the envoys took their leave, quiet discussion followed them out like a trailing mist. When the room emptied, only the King, Queen, and the three women remained.

Freija broke the silence. "They saw her. They may not admit it yet... but they saw her."

Kimiko sat on the table's edge, eyes dimming again. "Let them doubt me. As long as they act."

Frigid approached her slowly. She rested her hand on the table beside Kimiko's. "We'll act too. Together. But this isn't just about the world out there. It's about who we become when the world changes."

Freija added, her voice quieter, more grounded, "It already has. And I'm not sure who I'm becoming."

Kimiko looked up, meeting both their eyes.

"Then maybe it's time we find out."

The wind howled softly beyond the walls, carrying with it the promise of what lay ahead.

They stood together in silence, no longer just as warriors... but as women on the edge of transformation.

Outside, the storm held its breath. Tomorrow, they would begin.

The Journey Begins

The skies above Frostholm were unusually clear when the morning arrived, painted with streaks of lavender and silver, though the chill still lingered with teeth. A soft layer of powder blanketed the city like a silken shroud, muting the usual morning bustle. In the royal courtyard, preparations were nearly complete.

Frigid stood near the docking platform holding her double ended battle spear, her white cloak pulled tight around her shoulders. Her wings twitching with anticipation. Her gaze was fixed on the vessel that would carry them across the vast icy expanses and into the Eastern territories of Skarae. It wasn't a warship, but neither was it purely ceremonial – a hybrid-class diplomatic transport with reinforced hull plating and cloaking enchantments designed for travel through volatile climates.

Beside her, Freija inspected a crate of equipment. Her twin blades were sheathed across her back, and her expression was more serious than usual. She glanced up at her sister. "Everything ready on your end?"

Frigid nodded. "The Queen personally authorized our itinerary. The Parliament is watching closely. Every continent is either struggling to contain their disasters or waiting to see if we're walking into another myth come to life."

"We are," Freija said dryly. "But they wouldn't believe us until the sky split open."

A short distance away, Kimiko sat at the foot of the loading ramp, meditating. She was silent as ever, but her posture had changed since the bonding. The Gatekeeper within her had altered her very presence – an aura of calm intensity now radiated from her with subtle authority. The blue-white glow in her eyes had faded since the ritual, though the Frostheart charm around her neck shimmered with lingering energy.

As she watched the last of the supplies being loaded, her fingers brushed against the floor of the ramp. A pulse rippled up her arm – not pain, not discomfort, but sensation. Awareness.

She could feel it again.

Not just the Gatekeeper's presence within her, but something on the horizon. Something stirring.

Frigid approached her quietly. "You felt it again, didn't you?"

Kimiko gave a small nod while beginning to stand. "Yes. Like a storm gathering behind a wall. Not near. But not far enough."

Freija joined them, adjusting her sword harness. "Where first?"

Frigid produced a sealed parchment and unfolded the diplomatic charter. "We're expected at the Equatorial Tribunal on the Eastern Continent. Their governing council has reported tremors along their geothermal rift network. Some of their ceremonial shrines have begun leaking plasma fire. They think it's connected to their ancient fire deity, Tyrenka."

"Let me guess," Freija muttered. "The fire elemental."

"Most likely," Kimiko said. "The Gatekeeper agrees."

Freija raised a brow. "Wait – you spoke to him?"

Kimiko shook her head. "Not in words. But I know. When I ask questions inside my mind, I feel certainty or uncertainty in return. Emotion. Instinct. A kind of resonance. It's like asking the wind for direction and feeling it push back."

Frigid studied her carefully. "Can he speak directly?"

"Maybe," Kimiko said. "Or maybe he's waiting."

Freija let out a slow breath. "Let's hope he doesn't wait too long."

The group boarded the vessel as the engines began their hum of activation. Inside, the flight deck was already staffed by a small crew loyal to the Queen – engineers, navigators, and an experienced female Icelandian captain named Terina who had served under Glaciana during her early reign.

"Ready to depart on your command," Terina said from the helm.

Frigid took her seat at the diplomatic console. "Set course for the Equatorial Tribunal. Skarae the Eastern Continent."

Kimiko and Freija strapped into the co-pilot and support seats. As the vessel lifted off the pad, a low vibration coursed through the floor.

Through the viewport, Frostholm began to shrink beneath them, its icy spires retreating into the clouds.

Kimiko stared forward, eyes narrowing. "Something's coming. I can feel it waiting."

Freija glanced at her. "The fire elemental?"

Kimiko didn't answer.

Because it wasn't fear she felt.

It was recognition.

The journey had now begun.

Ash and Ember

The Cracked Horizon

The ship's descent was rough. Through the reinforced viewport, Skarae sprawled below them like a tapestry of ruin. What had once been a vibrant land of geothermal wonders and flowing lava rivers now smoldered under siege. Thick plumes of smoke clawed at the sky, casting a red-orange haze that obscured the sun. Pockets of flame bloomed across the rocky plains, while shattered villages and scorched groves marked the landscape in every direction.

"This... this isn't a disaster zone," Frigid muttered, clutching the edge of her seat. "It's a war zone."

Freija's face was set with grim resolve. "There's something here. I can feel it."

From her seat near the window, Kimiko's posture remained still, but the glow of her Frostheart charm had intensified. She inhaled deeply.

"It's the fire elemental," she said. "And it's awake."

The vessel touched down near the remains of a ravaged outpost. Terina gave them the go-ahead before powering down the ship's outer lights. The team disembarked quickly.

A guttural roar echoed in the distance – followed by another. Then the ground trembled.

Figures emerged through the smoke.

Golems – each six feet tall, burning with inner flame, formed from hardened magma and flickering embers. Dozens of them. Then hundreds. They marched through the haze with mechanical precision, setting fire to anything they passed.

Kimiko stepped forward, hands resting on the hilts of her twin katanas, her twin sai at her sides. Frigid's spear snapped open with a metallic ring. Freija's blades flared with cold light.

"Time to work," Freija growled.

Unleashed Fury

Freija launched into the sky with a single beat of her wings, blue trails cutting through the smoke as she zipped between burning towers. A fire golem raised an arm, hurling a searing chunk of molten rock toward the air.

Freija twisted midair, barely dodging the projectile, then dove downward like a missile. Her twin swords spun in opposite arcs, slamming into a golem's molten core. Ice burst from the impact, extinguishing its fiery light. It collapsed into blackened stone.

She streaked past three more, freezing one mid-step and cleaving another across its chest. She flipped sideways in midair, twisted into a corkscrew, and released a pulse of frost energy that froze two more where they stood.

On the ground, Frigid spun her double-ended spear in a sweeping arc, deflecting flame bursts time and time again. With every strike, her weapon channeled intense cold that counteracted the blazing heat. She moved with poise, sweeping flames away with calculated fury.

She slammed her spear into the chest of a charging golem, the impact flaring with ice and shattering its core. "Aim for their cores! Freeze them!" she shouted to the troops behind her. "Use cold – ice, water, frost spells! Heat won't harm them!"

Around her, Icelandian warriors surged forward. Many took to the skies like Freija and fought in coordinated formations. Spear-wielders formed protective walls while aerial units bombarded the golems from above, launching bursts of frost-infused energy. Two squads worked together, surrounding a trio of golems and lancing them with spears enchanted with glacial steel. With a final war cry, they brought the beasts down.

"Circle and split!" one warrior captain called. "Don't let them group! Use the wind!"

Frostcraft arrows, reinforced with elemental runes, shot through the haze from atop crumbled battlements, striking the joints and cores of the golems. Where enough ice clung, the creatures burst apart into harmless lava rock.

Twin Tempests

Another wave surged from the hills.

Frigid twirled her spear, sweeping three golems into a stumble before freezing them in place. But one broke through and lunged for her.

"Frigid, duck!" Freija screamed from above and launched downward, wings flared. She drove both swords into the golem's shoulders, releasing twin blasts of cold that erupted into a snowy explosion. The creature disintegrated with a hiss.

Freija landed beside her sister. "Remember the maneuver we used during the Twin Trials?"

Frigid gave a breathless smile. "You mean the Spiral Crescent?"

"Exactly." Freija responded laughing.

They shot into the air together, flying in mirrored spirals that circled a pack of five golems. As they ascended, frost magic condensed between them. When they crossed paths at the apex of their loop, they descended in tandem, forming a V-shaped attack with cold spears and blades flaring. The result was catastrophic. A burst of ice erupted from the impact zone, turning three golems into brittle fragments.

A fourth staggered. Frigid landed hard, thrusting her spear forward in a final jab that finished it. The twins locked eyes and grinned briefly.

"You've still got it," Frigid said.

"I never lost it," Freija replied, wings catching the air again.

The Edge of Control

Kimiko moved through the chaos like a shadow. Her katanas sang through the air, cutting down flaming foes with masterful precision. Every strike almost nothing against the molten golems except for a little distraction.

The fire golems were growing bolder, adapting. The fires flared higher. The air itself seemed to scream.

The Gatekeeper stirred.

She paused mid-swing as a pulse surged through her body. Her aura flickered – white-blue light cracking around her fingers. Her breath hitched.

111

Another golem lunged, and Kimiko turned with a roar, slicing it in half with frost energy now being part of her blade. The energy inside her trembled.

Emotion.

Not hers – but someone else's. She felt sorrow. Compassion. Desperation.

The Gatekeeper was feeling the suffering around them. Every scream, every lost home, every burning tree.

Kimiko staggered back. She dropped to one knee.

Frigid noticed first. "Kimiko?!"

Kimiko forced herself up. "I... I'm fine."

Freija fought her way to her side. "You don't look fine."

"It's the Gatekeeper," Kimiko said. "He... it... feels everything. Too much."

"You have to focus," Frigid said hovering nearby. "We need you."

Kimiko clenched her jaw, breathing deeply. The power steadied. The light at her fingertips dimmed.

"I'm okay," she said again, firmer this time.

Around them, fire golems continued to advance. Though dozens had fallen, more surged from the horizon.

"We can't hold this line forever," Freija muttered.

Kimiko stood slowly. "Then we find the source."

Freija nodded. "And end this."

Flames in the Mind

Even as Freija and Frigid led squads of Icelandian warriors through a flanking formation around the smoldering ridge, more fire golems surged forth from the molten caverns of the scorched earth. Their bodies glowed like molten steel, trailing flames in their wake. The air was so thick with heat that even the reinforced armor of the soldiers hissed and steamed with every breath.

Now Kimiko stood motionless. She stood atop a jagged outcrop of obsidian rock, her katana sheathed, eyes closed. Around her, chaos reigned. The Gatekeeper's energy shimmered faintly around her form, trailing like steam in the burning air. But inside her mind, there was only silence.

Until it wasn't.

They are in pain, the voice came – not as sound, but a wave of deep sorrow and truth. Not just the people, not just the soldiers screaming in agony as golems burned through the tree lines. But the trees themselves. The animals. The sky. Even the dirt beneath her boots trembled with anguish.

It was… overwhelming.

She staggered backward, clutching her head. A rush of memories, sensations, and raw, elemental emotion poured through her like a tsunami.

She felt the death of a thousand insects crushed under falling ash. The searing scream of a wolf engulfed in flame. The agony of each blade of grass incinerated in an instant. The hopelessness of every fallen warrior, of every fighter whose last breath never touched clean air again.

"No... no..." she whispered, knees buckling.

The Gatekeeper inside her pulsed harder. The power was responding to the trauma, flaring in her aura. Blue-white light burst from her skin in pulses, uncontrolled and wild. The glow in her eyes shimmered like the breaking of a dam. Her Frostheart charm pulsated rapidly in large bursts of light and energy.

From across the battlefield and several hundred feet above, Freija spotted her. Her wings snapped wider and she dove low, slicing through the sky with supernatural speed. Fire golems lunged from below, but her blades cut through them with icy arcs, extinguishing their cores with surgical strikes.

She landed beside Kimiko just as the ninja collapsed to one knee, gasping.

"Kimiko!" Freija shouted.

"Too much," Kimiko whispered. "I feel everything. Every death, every cry, every agony. I can't shut it out."

Freija dropped to one knee and gripped Kimiko's shoulders tightly her wings almost wrapping fully around Kimiko. "Listen to me. This isn't just you. You're carrying a spirit older than our civilizations. The Gatekeeper feels everything because it must. But you... you are still you. Anchor it. Don't let it drown you."

Tears welled in Kimiko's eyes, glowing faintly blue.

"You don't understand. It hurts. It hurts so much. I feel every life, every breath… every death."

Freija didn't falter. Her voice softened. "Yes, I do. Not like you. But I've seen pain. We all have. You remember the siege on Seraph's Reach?"

Kimiko blinked through the haze. "We lost eight of our own."

"And we held the line."

"The outpost on Krelos IV..."

"You took out a sentry tower with nothing but a length of cord and a stun dart," Freija said, smiling despite the smoke around them. "And what about Necra? You were the one who saved the galaxy from her tyranny. You, Kimiko!"

"This is different," Kimiko said. "I don't just feel for them now. I *am* them. I am the grass. The flame. The ash. And it's so much."

Freija cupped her friend's face. "Then be the other side too. Be the water. The wind. The balance. The Gatekeeper isn't just pain, Kimiko. He's peace. You just have to let him show you. Don't resist it."

Kimiko's body shuddered. The light flickered across her skin again.

Around them, the fire golems roared. Explosions of molten earth flared in the distance. But for a moment, there was only stillness between them.

The Gatekeeper's voice echoed once more inside her mind.

For every pain, there is healing. For every wound, there is restoration. You must endure in order to restore the balance.

Kimiko opened her eyes.

She saw the battlefield anew – not just the burning trees and broken stone, but the lives that remained. The warriors still fighting. The hope still flickering in every slash of Icelandian warrior's blade; the unrenowned spirit of an ice-shard spear thrown by an Icelandia fighter. In Frigid's brilliant defensive strikes that protected the wounded. In the defiance of every being that refused to fall.

Balance.

She rose slowly, and Freija stepped back, watching her carefully.

The energy around Kimiko stilled. The blue-white aura tightened into her skin. The pain didn't vanish – but it no longer overwhelmed. It was a part of her. And she would carry it.

"Let's finish this," Kimiko said.

Freija grinned. "Thought you'd never say it."

The two warriors turned back to the fray. The golems surged anew, and Kimiko drew her katana.

And this time, the fire would burn no more.

Embers on the Wind

The fire had scorched everything.

As dawn broke across the ash-dusted cliffs of Skarae, a sickly orange haze clung to the horizon. Blackened trees jutted like skeletal fingers toward a sky still glowing from the infernos that had torn through the region overnight. What little wildlife remained had gone silent. The earth was warm to the touch, pulsing with residual heat – as though the fires were not entirely gone.

The diplomatic vessel hovered at a safe distance above the worst of the burn zone, its stabilizers humming low as it slowly descended into the ruins of what had once been the village of Nyvareth. The landing skids touched down on scorched stones, kicking up clouds of soot and embers.

Frigid led the descent ramp, her white cloak pulled tight around her shoulders. Her gaze was fixed on the vessel's surroundings. It was worse than any of their reports. Nothing had survived. Beside her, Freija adjusted the straps of her frost-forged armor, her short white hair tousled from the shifting winds. Her cobalt-blue skin shimmered faintly in the early light. Kimiko came last, her dark figure contrasting sharply with her Icelandian companions. The Gatekeeper's presence lingered around her like an echo, silent but palpable.

Awaiting them near the ruins stood a squad of Icelandian warriors – each one blue-skinned, white-haired, and winged like Freija and Frigid. They were shorter, ranging between five and five-foot-five, but all were lithe and disciplined. Their froststeel armor was scorched in places but still held its sheen. Their captain, a stern-faced woman with braided white hair and a frostbrand scar along her cheek, stepped forward.

"I am Captain Syra of the Flamewatch," she said, her voice crisp. "We've been holding this line for days. The fire golems are retreating further into the Molten Scar. We believe that's where the source lies."

Frigid nodded. "We're here to help. The Queen sent us with full diplomatic and military sanction."

Syra's eyes shifted to Kimiko. "And the outsider? The one who bears the Gatekeeper?"

"I am Kimiko," the ninja said. "I serve Icelandia now."

Syra gave a small nod. "Then we'll see what your oath means in fire."

Two squads of Flamewatch moved into position behind their captain – each member wielding spears or glaives etched with frostrunes. Their stance was solid and eyes sharp.

Frigid gestured to the east. "Where's the last known trace of the elemental?"

"The Scar," Syra said. "Its presence is strongest there. But it changes the terrain as it moves – melting stone, creating tunnels. Our last patrol found scorched bones and nothing else."

The group advanced into the ruined terrain. Freija flew overhead in slow arcs, scouting ahead as her wings shimmered in the hot air. Kimiko walked just behind Frigid, silent as ever, but alert. Around her, the air shimmered with faint light from the Gatekeeper's aura.

As they passed through a shattered stone archway, Kimiko paused. Her hand reached for the Frostheart at her chest.

"It's close," she said.

"How close?" Frigid asked.

"Too close," Kimiko murmured.

The earth trembled.

They rushed forward as the path opened into a scorched basin. Dozens of fire golems stood in formation around a glowing obsidian platform. Their six-foot frames were hunched and jagged, fire bleeding from their cores and mouths. New ones emerged from molten vents along the walls.

"They're forming a guard ring," Freija said, landing beside the others. "They're waiting for something."

"The elemental," Kimiko said. "This is its seat of power."

Syra and her squads moved into battle formation. "We take the constructs now, before the elemental arrives."

Frigid nodded. "Agreed. Form a perimeter. Don't engage directly unless it attacks. Freija, aerial watch."

"I'm already ahead of you," Freija said, wings flaring as she rocketed skyward.

The Flamewatch split into squads of five, sweeping along the flanks. One group advanced cautiously through a melted tunnel on the right. Another moved up the ridge to gain high ground.

Frigid surged forward, frost trailing from her twin-ended spear. Her movements were elegant and practiced, each strike slicing through flaming limbs and core crystals. Beside her, a trio of warriors focused their frostshard lances into concentrated volleys, freezing and shattering one golem into burning rubble.

On the left flank, Freija streaked through the smoke like a bolt of lightning, moving at Mach 2 speeds. Her twin iceblades trailed frost trails behind her, cutting down three golems before she banked upward in a blur. She looped back around, spiraled through the air, and plunged straight into a cluster of them, smashing one apart with the full momentum of her dive.

"Frigid!" she called out. "Tactic Eleven?"

Frigid's eyes lit with recognition. "On my mark!"

The two sisters separated, then burst forward in a mirrored strike pattern – Freija from the air and Frigid from the ground. As they converged, their weapons moved in perfect synchronicity. Freija froze three golems mid-swing, and Frigid shattered them with a sweeping arc of her spear.

The Flamewatch took inspiration from their momentum. Several squads coordinated strikes with precision. Two warriors used their wings to flank a group of golems while a third froze their legs, collapsing them into a heap of burning rock.

But for every golem destroyed, two more emerged.

Captain Syra shouted above the din, "Aim for the core! Frost disables them fastest!"

The warning traveled quickly. More warriors began drawing rune-infused frost knives, targeting the golem cores. The tide held for a moment.

Then another wave came.

"We can't hold them forever," Frigid grunted.

"No," Kimiko said, stepping forward. "But we can hold them long enough."

She unsheathed her katana, the blade singing as it caught the air. The glow around her brightened – Gatekeeper stirring.

The battle for the Scar had begun.

And the fire elemental was almost here.

The Flame That Weeps

The cavern's entrance loomed ahead, glowing with the pulsing crimson light of magma veins that pulsed like the heartbeat of a wounded beast. Kimiko and the Icelandian warriors, led by Freija and Frigid, formed a perimeter, wings flared, weapons drawn, holding the line as waves of fire golems surged from the broken earth. Shards of obsidian clashed with glacial steel, and the air was thick with steam, ash, and the roar of battle.

"Push forward!" Freija shouted, spinning through the air with deadly grace. Her twin ice blades flashed in the smoke, extinguishing three fire golems in a single sweeping arc.

Frigid soared above the battlefield, her double-headed spear slicing through the air with precision. She landed beside her sister, frost trailing from her weapon with each strike. "We need an opening! Give Kimiko a path!"

The warriors heard the call and tightened formation, carving a temporary channel through the inferno. A dozen golems fell beneath coordinated attacks – sweeping flurries of cold magic, synchronized ice-bolts, and blade strikes. For a moment, the fire receded.

Kimiko, waiting at the rear of the battlefront, opened her eyes. They shimmered blue-white, barely human. She felt the Gatekeeper stirring, guiding her forward. The Frostheart pendant around her neck pulsed in time with her heartbeat – or was it the Gatekeeper's?

Without a word, she sprinted forward into the newly formed corridor. The Icelandian warriors held the flanks, closing ranks behind her. Fire golems tried to reform, but Freija and Frigid slammed into them with renewed fury, determined to give Kimiko the space she needed.

The deeper Kimiko moved, the more the temperature rose. Ash rained from the cavern ceiling. Her vision blurred with heat, but the Gatekeeper's energy surged inside her, keeping her steady.

At the heart of the cavern, she found it.

The fire elemental.

It hovered in the center of a magma chamber, suspended above a pit of lava. Its body was vast – a constantly shifting humanoid form of flame and molten stone, crowned with a mane of fire and eyes that glowed like dying stars. Its roars were not of rage… but sorrow.

Kimiko stepped forward, sword undrawn. Her aura flared.

The elemental turned.

"Why do you chase me?" it hissed. Its voice was like burning wind. "Why do you seek my silence?"

Kimiko didn't answer. She let the Gatekeeper rise.

Her eyes rolled back, glowing brighter. Her limbs relaxed, her posture shifting from warrior to Vessel. The Gatekeeper took over, and her aura exploded with light.

A wave of blue-white energy erupted from her chest. The chamber shuddered.

"I come not to silence you," the Gatekeeper's voice said, now layered with Kimiko's, as though two beings spoke in unison. "I come to balance you."

The fire elemental recoiled. "You are his Vessel... the heart-bound one. But you are not of the old blood."

"This Vessel is royal by right of soul… by heart… by lineage… beyond this world," the Gatekeeper replied. "Your grief has festered into fury. Your isolation has burned into madness. Let me share your pain."

The fire elemental shrieked and launched a pillar of flame. The Gatekeeper raised Kimiko's hand. A sigil of ancient Icelandian origin flared into being, and the fire dissolved into harmless light.

"No more lies," the elemental howled.

They clashed.

Flame and frost collided. The cavern became a battlefield of energy. The Gatekeeper, through Kimiko, summoned glacial walls, mirrored shields, and spirals of pure magical force. The elemental responded with waves of heat, molten spikes, and firestorms that danced like living creatures.

But it wasn't a battle to destroy.

It was a battle to understand.

As they fought, the Gatekeeper sent tendrils of light into the elemental's body. Not weapons, but memories. Visions.

The elemental's past poured through Kimiko.

A time before war. When it danced through volcanic plains with other elementals. When fire was a giver of warmth, of life, of passion.

Then came the bindings. The sanctums. The fear.

Kimiko felt it all. Saw it all. She trembled, crying out silently as the Gatekeeper bore the pain of thousands years of solitude. Through her, it became human. Real. Tangible.

"You do not have to burn alone," the Gatekeeper said.

The fire elemental began to shrink, its flames dimming.

"I am forgotten," it whispered. "I was left. Buried. Used."

"So was I," the Gatekeeper answered. "But now, I remember. And I remember you."

They reached out to one another.

The cavern floor erupted in light. Runes swirled into a sanctum beneath the elemental. A new sanctum – not of pain, but of peace. A sphere of crystal and obsidian formed, laced with runes of containment and empathy.

The elemental made no move to flee.

As it was drawn into the new sanctum, the final emotion it gave was not fear, but release.

And all of it passed through Kimiko.

She felt the grief. The rage. The loneliness. But also, the gratitude. The warmth. The acceptance.

The crystal sealed.

And the cavern fell silent.

Back on the surface, the remaining fire golems crumbled. One by one, they collapsed into flickers of fire, then ash. A strange breeze swept over the battlefield, cool and clean.

Freija looked up, catching the change. "She did it," she whispered.

Frigid, breathing hard and singed at the edges, exhaled. "Kimiko..."

Deep within the cavern, Kimiko collapsed to her knees. Her body trembled, sweat and tears streaking her face. Her aura dimmed, but the light in her eyes still flickered with the Gatekeeper's spark.

She was no longer the same.

And the true cost of that transformation had yet to be understood.

The Vessel's Breath

The battlefield was still, save for the soft hiss of cooling rock and the occasional crackle of dying embers. The fire golems had collapsed like puppets with cut strings, their molten cores extinguished the instant the elemental had been subdued. In their place were trails of scorched glass and crumbling ash, fading slowly beneath the return of Icelandia's eternal frost.

But Kimiko had not emerged.

Freija stood at the mouth of the cavern, her wings twitching with tension. She had waited exactly two minutes – long enough for most of the flames to die down, not long enough for the knot in her stomach to loosen. Her eyes narrowed.

"No," she muttered. "That's enough waiting."

Without another word, she kicked off the ground vertically, wings spreading wide as the icy wind caught her immediately. She arched up in a powerful loop, gaining altitude before plunging into the cavern mouth like a dive-bombing falcon. The wind howled past her ears, her body a blur of motion as the dark rock walls narrowed around her.

Frigid followed just seconds behind, more reserved in her descent but equally focused. "Stay close to the wall," she called out. "There's debris falling!"

They wove through collapsing stone and smoke, darting around burning wreckage and pockets of steam. The deeper they went, the more the air shimmered with heat – but something else, too. A pulsing presence. A heartbeat in the rock.

Then they saw her.

Kimiko knelt in the center of the cavern, bathed in the aftermath of magical convergence. The floor beneath her was scorched but cooling rapidly, crystalline frost growing in elegant webs from the tips of her fingers to the stone around her. Her body trembled, shoulders rising and falling in uneven bursts. Her katana lay forgotten at her side, and her hands were pressed to the ground as if she had fallen from a great height.

She was crying.

Silent tears streamed down her cheeks – blue, glowing faintly in the darkness. Her chest heaved. Her lips trembled in a whisper of laughter. She was smiling. And yet, her eyes shimmered with the aftershock of something unfathomable.

Freija landed hard beside her and dropped to one knee. "Kimiko!" she gasped, reaching forward. "Are you – are you hurt?"

Kimiko's only answer was a soft, gasping breath.

"Air…" she whispered. "I need… air."

Frigid landed on the opposite side. "We're taking her out of here. Now."

Freija quickly sheathed the fallen katana. Then, without hesitation, both sisters took an arm. Kimiko felt strangely weightless – either from exhaustion or the lingering magic still clinging to her aura. Her Frostheart charm pulsed bright, beating rhythmically in sync with her labored breathing.

Freija's wings flared with a gust of power. "Hold tight," she said. "We'll have you breathing clean sky in no time."

Frigid looking into Freija's eyes, "1… 2… 3… Go!" They launched in unison, soaring back up through the cavern with Kimiko between them. Her body dangled slightly, but her head tilted back to take in the rising arc of the stone walls, the swirling mist, the silver-blue light breaking through the upper crevices.

It was beautiful, in a terrifying way.

They burst free into open sky moments later, the wind biting and pure. Kimiko coughed, dragging a deep lung full of cold air. Frigid and Freija brought her down gently on a patch of unburnt snow just beyond the cavern entrance.

Kimiko collapsed to her knees again, but this time the air was clear. Her body stopped shaking. The glow from her Frostheart slowed to a calm rhythm.

She looked up, looking into Freija's eyes. "I was… inside myself," she murmured. "Watching."

Freija frowned. "Watching what?"

Kimiko's gaze drifted past her, lost in memory. "Everything."

She brought her hand to her chest. "The Gatekeeper… when he took control, I wasn't gone. I was still there. A passenger. I felt him reach out to the fire elemental. Not with anger. Not with dominance. But with sorrow. With understanding. He didn't destroy it."

Frigid knelt beside her. "What did he do?"

Kimiko looked at them both – her teammates, her friends – and finally let the tears fall freely.

"He soothed it. He took its pain… and felt it. Absorbed it. Every scream, every heartbeat, every moment of loneliness that fire had endured for many millennia. He felt it all… and then showed it something else. Peace. Compassion. Balance."

She touched her heart again. "He showed it… love."

Neither Freija nor Frigid spoke. The only sound was the wind shifting the snow nearby and the low moan of the earth as the fires below finally died.

"I felt all of it," Kimiko whispered. "As if it were my own. The rage. The isolation. The agony… then the calm. The elemental didn't want to fight. It was scared. It didn't know how to stop burning. He showed it how."

Freija sat beside her, slowly removing one glove and placing her bare hand over Kimiko's.

"I've never heard you speak like this," she said softly. "Not in all the time we've fought together."

Kimiko gave her a watery smile. "I've never felt like this. It's… terrifying. But also… freeing."

Frigid stared at her with a mix of awe and concern. "You didn't just bind with a spirit. You became a part of something else. Something ancient and kind. But it's still you, Kimiko. It chose you."

Kimiko nodded, wiping her face. "I know. And I'll carry it. For as long as I must."

They sat together in the snow, the fires behind them long extinguished. Above, the sky opened a little wider, letting streaks of faint sunlight pierce the veil of clouds.

For the first time in hours, the land was quiet.

And for the first time in her life, Kimiko felt like she was no longer just a blade, a shadow, or a weapon.

She was something more.

Cracks in the World

The journey across the ocean was silent at first.

After the confrontation beneath the scorched earth of Skarae, the diplomatic vessel soared through pale skies, banking eastward over the Sea of Vapors. Below them, the churning waters stretched to the horizon – dark and tumultuous, reflecting the unrest within the hearts of those onboard. A few flecks of sunlight pierced the clouds, casting golden shards across the sea, but even that light seemed uncertain.

Kimiko sat near the forward viewport, her eyes distant, the Frostheart charm at her neck now pulsing faintly, steady as a drumbeat. Though her body had recovered, her mind was still tangled in the aftershock of what had occurred. The Gatekeeper had acted through her – and it had changed something deep inside.

Freija stood just behind her, arms crossed, wings twitching faintly as she studied the coastlines approaching on the horizon. "How much longer?" she asked over her shoulder.

Frigid was seated at the navigation station beside Terina, the ship's pilot. Her voice was measured. "We'll reach the edge of Sommara in ten minutes. Preliminary scans show unstable fault lines across the southern lowlands. Cities once perched on cliffs have collapsed. Farmlands have disappeared into sinkholes."

"It's worse than we thought," Terina muttered, adjusting the controls.

Freija turned toward Kimiko, watching the Gatekeeper's Vessel as she sat in stillness. The glow in Kimiko's eyes had dimmed but not vanished. She looked calmer now, yet there was a distance in her presence – as if she were sharing space with someone else. Or something else.

Frigid noticed it too. "Is he still... active?" she asked carefully.

Kimiko nodded slowly, her voice soft. "He rests... for now. But the land beneath us is screaming. He hears it, even in silence."

The diplomatic vessel descended through heavy gray clouds, and as they pierced the last misty veil, the Western Continent of Sommara unfolded before them – fractured, broken, gashed open by titanic forces.

Massive sinkholes pockmarked the land like scars. Forests once proud and green had crumbled into deep fissures, and whole cities had buckled inward, swallowed by the hungry earth. The sky itself felt heavy here – drawn low by the suffering etched across the land.

From her seat, Kimiko whispered, "The earth weeps."

As they descended further, small pockets of life came into view: temporary shelters, huddled groups of blue-skinned Icelandian people tending to their injured companions or surveying crumbled ruins. Frigid's brow furrowed. "They're barely holding together."

"We need to land," Freija said. "These people need help before we even find the elemental."

Frigid nodded. "Agreed. There's a stable ridge near one of the less-affected towns. We can make contact with their local council and assess the situation before moving into the deeper fault lines."

The ship adjusted course, banking toward the fractured region's edge. As they flew, Kimiko leaned closer to the viewport, her voice distant.

"There's something else here. Deeper. Not like the fire elemental. This one doesn't burn. It waits. It watches. It judges."

Freija stepped beside her. "Can you tell where?"

Kimiko closed her eyes. "Not yet. But soon."

The ship slowed as they approached a makeshift landing pad constructed from salvaged stone and reinforced metal. Local Icelandian guards with frost-edged spears and worn cloaks waited to receive them, wings furled tightly against the dust-laden wind.

As the landing struts touched the cracked stone, the ship shuddered slightly – another tremor rolling beneath the continent's broken skin.

Frigid stepped forward, voice calm but authoritative. "Let's meet the locals. We'll need all the information we can get before we go further into this... fractured heartland."

Freija looked to Kimiko. "You up for this?"

Kimiko rose slowly, her posture straightening, the faintest shimmer of energy gathering around her limbs. "I'm ready."

Outside, the earth cracked again in the distance, the land itself shifting like a restless beast beneath their feet.

The wind was gritty, dry, and cold as the trio stepped down from the vessel. Several of the Icelandian guards saluted Frigid and Freija, then turned to stare with cautious reverence at Kimiko. The glow of the Frostheart pendant and the residual blue shimmer in her aura marked her as something more than a mere traveler.

A local official – barely older than Freija, his face lined with soot and worry – stepped forward, wings slightly unfurled in greeting. "Princess Frigid. Princess Freija. Welcome to town of Daelstone."

"Thank you," Frigid said, grasping the official's forearm in solidarity. "We've heard about the damage. We want to help."

The man – Varen, as he introduced himself – led them through the hastily assembled town square. It had once been a ceremonial plaza, but now it was filled with tents, makeshift kitchens, and medics treating the wounded.

"The tremors began four weeks ago," Varen explained. "At first, we thought it was just the seasonal shifts beneath the range. But then the sinkholes started. Deep. Endless. Whole houses and farms swallowed overnight."

Another elder stepped forward – a woman with piercing silver eyes. "And then we saw them. Creatures. Hulking, stone-like things. Golems. They rose from the fissures and struck anything near."

Freija frowned. "Earth golems. Like the fire constructs."

"They don't speak," Varen said, "but it's like they're searching. Digging."

Kimiko listened quietly, her hand resting against a fallen pillar. Her eyes narrowed slightly.

"They're not digging," she said. "They're trying to reach something. Or someone."

Frigid turned to the crowd of survivors. "Has there been any sign of a larger entity? Something different?"

Varen hesitated, then nodded. "There's a fault line beyond the river. No one goes near it now. The ground sings, Princess. Like... like a chorus of stone moaning. It drives animals mad."

Kimiko's head tilted. "That's where we'll find it."

A silence fell over the group.

"We leave at first light," Frigid said. "We'll bring provisions, gear, and as many volunteers as are willing to help."

Several warriors stepped forward immediately – young men and women with determination in their eyes. Icelandians who refused to watch their land fall without a fight.

Freija offered a smile. "Let's remind this land that we don't crack easily."

And as the last rays of daylight dipped below the fractured horizon, the group returned to the vessel to rest – aware that the next confrontation would bring them face to face with the next elemental threat.

And Kimiko, still bearing the Gatekeeper's presence, closed her eyes and listened.

Beneath the ground, the earth called. And she would soon answer.

Tremors Beneath the Earth

The sun rose slowly over the fractured coastline of Sommara, painting the broken terrain in pale hues of blue and gold. Now, the team gathered again at first light.

Frigid rubbed the fatigue from her eyes as she stepped out into the crisp morning air. A cool breeze off the ocean brought with it the tang of salt and ash. The landscape around them remained unsettling – earth cracked in long fault lines, buildings half-swallowed by the ground, and a silence that felt too heavy, too watched.

Freija walked up beside her with a rustle of wings, hair tousled from sleep but eyes sharp. "Sleep well?"

"Barely," Frigid muttered. "The ground trembled twice during the night. Not strong, but enough to keep me alert."

Kimiko emerged last, her expression unreadable but her movements were slower. Not tired – focused. She had sensed something during the night but chose not to speak of it yet.

Below the bluff, the camp was beginning to stir. Survivors emerged from makeshift shelters, soldiers tended to weapons and patrol routes, and steam curled from morning cookfires. The scent of stone and smoke mingled in the air.

They descended together into the encampment.

The locals were all Icelandian, blue-skinned with white hair, but they bore the marks of a harsher existence. Many were younger, leaner, their armor cobbled together from pieces of salvaged gear and ceramic plates. Their leader – a middle-aged warrior with braided silver hair and a long scar across her temple – stepped forward with a respectful bow of her wings.

"I am Captain Virell of Stonehold. You are from Frostholm?"

"I am Frigid," she replied, inclining her head. "And this is my sister Freija. Our companion is Kimiko."

"The one they say carries the Gatekeeper," Virell said, her voice hushed but not fearful. She looked Kimiko over carefully. "You are an off-worlder, but we are grateful for your help."

"What happened here?" Freija asked.

Virell gestured toward the crumbling cliffs. "Three weeks ago, tremors began shaking the coast. Then sinkholes opened. At first, we thought it was tectonic instability. But then the golems emerged. Massive creatures, forged of stone and root, their eyes glowing like molten ore. They tore through the valley, crushed our defenses, and vanished underground. We've held them back since – barely."

"Where are they now?" Kimiko asked.

Virell motioned inland. "There's a series of caves beyond the ridge. We think they come from there – when the tremors grow strongest, they rise from the earth like giants from a forgotten age."

Kimiko's eyes narrowed. "Then that's where the stone elemental is."

Virell nodded gravely. "We've sent scouts, but none have returned. The land resists entry. Pathways collapse. Shadows move where there should be none."

Freija exhaled. "Sounds like a party."

Frigid crossed her arms. "We'll need a full map of the region, everything you've charted since this began. Safe zones, chokepoints, seismic patterns – anything that might help us plan a path through."

"I'll have my second deliver it," Virell said. "You'll want to speak with Councilor Teman as well. He's our historian and geologist. He's been researching old myths about this land since the tremors started."

As they were led through the camp, Kimiko walked slightly apart, feeling the pulse of the Gatekeeper – faint now, but flickering. Something ancient stirred beneath the stone, a force that felt... grounded. Patient. Immovable.

A chill threaded down her spine.

Later that morning, Frigid and Freija stood over a large table in the command tent with Teman, a short scholar draped in worn ceremonial robes. The man pushed a set of layered parchment maps forward with trembling fingers.

"These caves?" Frigid asked, pointing to a hollow just east of a ridge marked in red.

"Yes," Teman said. "They form a natural sink basin. The cave system has long been considered sacred. We believed it to be dormant, the resting place of an 'earthen watcher.' A being said to sleep until the world forgets its own balance."

Freija scoffed. "Sounds familiar."

"Have any ancient bindings been recorded?" Frigid asked.

Teman nodded. "Two or three millennia ago, perhaps longer. There are carvings beneath the old monastery at the ridge's edge. They speak of a 'Heart of Stone' – one of four elemental forces meant to keep the world rooted in harmony."

Kimiko stepped forward. "And if it's awakening now…"

Teman's voice dropped. "Then we are far out of balance."

They fell into silence, the wind outside tugging at the tent seams like unseen fingers.

Freija clenched her jaw. "We'll scout the caves at mid-day. No one enters the core until we understand what we're facing."

"Agreed," Frigid said. "And tell your warriors to prepare. If the stone golems rise again, we'll need to hold the line."

Teman hesitated, then added quietly, "We don't know what will greet you inside. But we do know this – the stone elemental does not rage like fire or scream like wind. It waits. It watches. And when it moves… it moves to crush."

As mid-day approached, Kimiko sat alone on a ledge overlooking the cracked valley. The Frostheart charm glowed faintly against her skin. Within her, the Gatekeeper stirred – but offered no words. Only presence.

A pulse. A heartbeat. A weight.

Balance, she reminded herself. That's what I carry.

Stone and Strategy

The midday sun hung low in the sky, casting long shadows over the jagged cliffs of Sommara. Though the light was pale, it gleamed off the frost-rimed edges of the mountains, creating an almost eerie stillness as the strike team pressed forward. Frigid, Freija, Kimiko, and a contingent of Icelandian warriors now marched steadily toward the rumored cavern.

Frigid led the group, flanked by two local warrior-captains, including Captain Virell. Their white wings folded tightly over their tattered battle cloaks, the Icelandians bore expressions of grim resolve. Though all Icelandians shared the same blue-toned skin, cobalt-colored wings, and white hair, the Western Continent had hardened these fighters into tougher, battle-worn soldiers. Their armor was patched and scarred, their blades well-used.

Freija walked a few paces behind her sister, her eyes scanning the ridges and slopes. Her twin frostblades hung across her back, icy condensation rising from their hilts with each breath of wind. Kimiko followed quietly, her expression unreadable. The Frostheart charm at her neck pulsed slowly – like a distant heartbeat, or a warning. Her hands rested lightly on her sai at her waist, not drawn.

"This should be the entrance," one of the warrior-captains said, motioning to a jagged opening between two cliff walls. A path of broken stone led deeper into the gloom.

The group slowed. The mouth of the cavern yawned wide before them – dark, cold, and ominously still. Moss-covered stones framed the edges like jagged teeth, and faint vibrations rolled from within. Frigid's purple Frostheart began to beat wildly, a rhythmic throbbing against her chest.

"Weapons ready," Frigid commanded.

No sooner had they crossed the threshold than the first of the stone golems emerged. Towering ten feet tall, the golems appeared as walking statues – hulking constructs of basalt and granite, with runes etched into their limbs that glowed with dim orange fire. Their footsteps shook the earth.

"Positions!" Freija barked. Her own Frostheart flared in sync.

The Icelandian warriors fanned out into a wide formation, forming overlapping arcs of defense. The golems charged.

Frigid dashed forward, spinning her double-ended spear in a deadly blur. She struck the side of the first golem with precision... only for the tip to glance off harmlessly with a small spark, leaving no mark.

Freija launched into the air, wings slicing the mist. Her twin frostblades slashed down against another golem's back... sparks, and nothing more. The creature didn't even flinch.

More golems emerged from walls and cracks, slow, unstoppable juggernauts of stone. Warriors engaged with discipline and desperation. Ice axes shattered. Magic-tipped blades sparked. Shields crumpled.

"Pull back!" Frigid shouted. She jabbed her spear again getting the same result.

A call rang from the rear.

"Wait! I might have something!" Orrik, an older Icelandian scholar, sprinted toward them with a pack bouncing on his back.

"In one of my physics lessons," he gasped, "we experimented with sealed vessels filled with water. When frozen, they cracked apart... stone won't fare better! You see water expands when it freezes"

Frigid's eyes narrowed. Her Frostheart throbbed like a war drum. "You're saying we soak them, get water in their joints, and then freeze them?"

"Yes! The pressure from inside should..."

"Freija! Ocean water!"

"On it!" Freija turned to a team of aerial warriors. "Wings up! Bring water! Buckets, sacks, anything!"

The winged warriors launched into the sky in formation. A cinematic sweep of wings filled the horizon. Below, others provided cover. Arrows and frostbursts distracted the golems.

Minutes later, the first wave of seawater arrived. Warriors drenched one of the golems from head to toe. Freija darted in, blades glinting.

Frigid hurled her spear now glowing with concentrated frostburst energy. It struck the soaked golem.

CRACK.

Ice spidered through the golem's body. Its limbs buckled. With a groan, it collapsed into a heap of shards of stone and ice.

"It worked!" Frigid yelled.

Cheers erupted.

But more golems came. A second wave. Faster. Their runes now glowed brighter.

On a ledge above, Freija struck again... her two swords clanged together to counter an attack from one of the stone golems. A reverberated tone echoed from the clang of the two swords..

The golem before her flinched.

She struck again, this time with intent. Flat of one blade against the base of the other. A sharp resonance rang out. The golem twitched again.

She struck a third time. The tone pierced the air. The golem's torso fractured... then burst.

"Resonant frequency!" she called. "Use your side weapons... create sound! It disrupt their structure!"

Frigid grabbed a dagger and struck it against her spear near the base. Her Frostheart flared. The golem before her trembled... then shattered.

Warriors adapted quickly. Daggers met blades. Staffs clanged against shields. The air filled with metallic song.

Kimiko watched from the cliffside. Her body glowed faintly. The Gatekeeper within her stirred... quiet, present. She stepped forward.

One golem broke past the line, heading for a wounded warrior. Kimiko moved like a shadow.

She drew one sai, struck it against the rocky floor, then tapped it gently against the golem's arm. The Frostheart charm at her neck pulsed.

The golem stopped.

Kimiko closed her eyes. Her other sai slid from its sheath. She struck the hilts together.

Piiiiiinnnnnng.

A chime like wind through crystal.

The golem's arm cracked, then collapsed.

She stepped back. No flourish. No anger. Only balance.

Virell and her warriors fought with grim efficiency. One warrior splashed a golem mid-charge. Another created a shimmering wall of frost. Two others slammed metal bars into opposing sides of a golem's legs, it shattered at the knees.

Freija dove and pulled a warrior from beneath a crumbling cliff just in time.

Frigid coordinated from the center, her Frostheart pulsing brighter with each tactical call. "Left flank – resonance only! Center, soak and strike! Wings, keep overhead clear!"

Through it all, the Frostheart charms of the three warriors lit the battlefield… three beacons of rhythm and resonance.

The battle was far from over, but unity had formed. Tactics had adapted. And against creatures born of earth and time, the Icelandians refused to break.

Kimiko stood silently as stone shattered around her, hands loose at her sides, the glow of the Gatekeeper humming faintly beneath her skin.

This was not rage. This was not vengeance.

This was balance.

And they were winning.

The Echo Beneath

The mouth of the deeper cavern loomed like a wound in the mountainside, dark and pulsing with quiet tremors. The stony path that led them here had been narrow, slick with condensation, and lined with crumbled ruins partially reclaimed by nature. Whatever civilization once dwelled in this place had long been buried beneath layers of silence.

Frigid stepped forward first, spear in hand, eyes narrowing at the runes carved around the archway. They were faint and worn but familiar in style to those she'd seen during her studies of early Icelandian architecture. Not Parliament-era – not even royal – but ancient. Pre-unification.

"These markings," she murmured, trailing her fingers across a spiral glyph. "They're not warnings. They're… prayers."

Freija joined her, blades drawn but idle at her sides. "Prayers to what?"

Frigid glanced over her shoulder. "To the earth itself. To the protector that once kept this region safe from flood and famine. Before it turned on them."

Behind them, Kimiko remained quiet. She stood still at the threshold, her hands resting lightly on the hilts of her sai at her waist. Her Frostheart pendant throbbed slowly, the blue-white pulse echoing like a heartbeat. The Gatekeeper within stirred, but not with urgency.

With reverent steps, they entered.

The cavern yawned open into a vast underground gallery. Tall stone columns rose toward a ceiling lost in darkness, each one carved with the likeness of armored sentinels. The air was cool but heavy. Every breath tasted of dust, minerals, and something else – a weight of time, compressed and unyielding.

"No fire damage, no collapses," Frigid noted. "This place has been undisturbed for millennia."

"Feels more like a tomb than a stronghold," Freija muttered. Her eyes scanned the shadows.

As they moved deeper, their footsteps echoed strangely, distorted by the acoustics of the chamber. The sound bounced and folded in on itself, becoming whispers, almost voices. Kimiko paused.

"You hear that?" Kimiko asked softly.

Frigid turned. "The echoes?"

"No. The silence between them. It's too still." Kimiko pressed her hand to the ground. The moment her bare palm touched the stone... a vision flickered.

A flash.

The cavern was filled with primitive rocky people – stone-skinned, wingless, robed in earthen tones. They moved in silence, heads bowed toward a massive statue in the center of the gallery. The statue bore a humanoid form, towering and androgynous, with arms outstretched in both welcome and warning. Its eyes were blindfolded, its chest open to reveal a heart made of quartz.

The vision passed.

Kimiko's breathing quickened. "This place was a sanctuary."

Frigid stepped beside her. "A shrine to the Stone Elemental. Before it turned?"

They approached the statue at the chamber's center. Though chipped and weathered, it stood nearly fifteen feet tall. Moss crept up its legs, and cracks had formed along the outstretched arms, but it retained its majesty.

A low vibration thrummed beneath their feet.

Freija frowned. "That's not the wind."

Kimiko stepped forward again. The Gatekeeper stirred. She could feel him... listening. And then something shifted. Not outside – inside her. The Gatekeeper shared a fragment of memory.

A kingdom once ruled from below, not above. Laws carved into stone, upheld by unbending will. Peace kept not by force, but by endurance.

Then betrayal. A ruler's promise broken. The elemental, once a guardian of wisdom, retreated into itself. Its sleep was not peace. It was mourning.

Kimiko blinked back tears.

"It wasn't just anger that drove it to violence," she said quietly. "It was heartbreak."

Frigid's brow furrowed. "You mean... it was abandoned?"

"Used," Kimiko corrected. "Betrayed by the very ones it protected."

Freija walked a slow circle around the statue. "Then how do we reach something that's decided the world isn't worth saving anymore?"

The floor trembled harder. Dust fell from the high arches. A rumble echoed from deeper in the tunnels.

Kimiko stood, her eyes glowing faintly. "We show it that not all promises are broken. That not all voices forget."

Another tremor shook the chamber. The statue's blindfold cracked.

Frigid raised her spear. "We don't have much time. That wasn't just an echo. That was a call."

They turned toward the sound.

Deep beneath the earth, something ancient and heavy was waking.

And it remembered the weight of betrayal.

The Weight of Ages

The chamber of the stone elemental was more ancient than anything Kimiko had ever seen. Even deeper than the first vault beneath Mount Solance, the cavern that opened before her was vast and solemn, carved not by magic, but time itself. Stalactites hung like jagged fangs from the ceiling, and wide pillars of petrified mineral had formed where water had once dripped for centuries without pause. The room pulsed with an oppressive, silent energy. Even before stepping fully inside, Kimiko could feel it. The weight.

She entered alone, boots echoing across a floor smoothed by millennia. The Gatekeeper stirred within her... not warning, not alarm, but a quiet readiness. Her Frostheart charm glowed with an unsteady light, as if reacting to something too vast for comprehension. The air grew heavier with every step, pressing down on her shoulders like unseen stone.

The chamber's center held a dais surrounded by carved rings in the ground, like the ripple marks of ancient seismic waves. Kimiko didn't need to be told where the elemental was. She could feel it... a slow, endless pressure in her chest, like gravity deepening with each breath.

From the silence, the elemental began to rise.

Not with speed, but with the inevitable force of tectonic movement. Sediment and obsidian peeled from the cavern floor, forming into the towering figure of a colossus – twenty feet tall, its limbs carved with spiral runes and buried histories. Glowing amber veins ran like molten rivers beneath its cracked skin. Its face bore no mouth, no eyes, only the faint suggestion of features shaped by seismic memory.

And then the pain of betrayal began.

Not her pain. The elemental's.

The Gatekeeper flared, and Kimiko's mind was pulled inward. She saw fragments... visions pressed into the earth like fossils:

...A thriving subterranean city built around the elemental's shrine, stone-voiced hymns echoing through the deep halls...

...A treaty signed aboveground, a promise to honor the elemental's counsel...

...A betrayal. The aboveground kingdoms, fearful of its power, sealing it away beneath layers of iron and ash...

...Many millennia of silence.

The elemental had not been imprisoned by chains... but by neglect.

Kimiko collapsed to her knees, overcome. Her breath hitched, her heart racing. The sorrow she felt was vast and unfathomable... a geological grief that had outlasted empires.

Outside, Frigid shouted orders as the landslide worsened. Stones the size of beasts crashed down the slope, some cracking open like eggshells as they struck the outer defenses. Freija's teams scrambled to form ice barriers and flying diversions. Frigid herself stood at the southern ridge, wielding her frost-forged spear like a commander of storms.

"Shift the formation! Keep the center line clear! We need more bodies on the north drop, now!" she roared.

A tremor shook the ground, not from the mountain, but from within. Frigid turned toward the cavern entrance. "Kimiko..."

Inside, Kimiko remained slumped, trembling. Her eyes glowed faintly, tears trailing down her cheeks. The elemental's presence was overpowering.

She didn't speak, she mouthed the words: *It's mourning.*

Frigid spread her wings bursting through the threshold into the cavern, drawn by the elemental's rising aura and the flickering of Kimiko's Frostheart. She slowed only slightly before crossing the circle of carved stone, dropping to Kimiko's side.

"Kimiko! What's wrong?" Frigid asked, panic in her voice.

Kimiko couldn't speak. She could only feel. Her body was not hers – it was a conduit, a mirror. Her fingers clawed at the floor, and her breath came in ragged gasps.

"It's the elemental," she choked out. "It's... it's grieving. I can feel it. It's been buried alive for many millennia. It doesn't know if it wants to sleep or scream."

Frigid knelt beside her, pulling her close. She wrapped her arms around Kimiko's shoulders, her cool aura providing a contrast to the warmth surging through the stone.

"You don't have to carry this alone," she whispered.

Kimiko sobbed. Not from pain. From empathy. "He just wanted to serve. To hold the world together. And they buried him... They buried him for it."

Frigid held her tighter. "Then we remind him that the world still needs him. That he's not forgotten."

The Gatekeeper's energy surged again, flaring outward through Kimiko like a ripple of truth.

Balance.

The elemental stepped forward, stone shoulders shifting like tectonic plates. Slowly, deliberately, it extended one massive arm toward Kimiko, its hand opening. The gesture was not one of attack, but of offering.

Kimiko breathed through her shudders and looked to Frigid. Her voice came soft but certain. "Come with me. Take my hand."

Frigid blinked through her worry but obeyed, slipping her hand into Kimiko's. Their fingers clasped tightly... warmth and cold united. Together, they approached the elemental.

Kimiko stepped forward first. With reverence, she placed her palm against the elemental's massive outstretched finger. Her hand was tiny by comparison, but the contact sent a wave of warmth and grounding through the chamber.

She turned her head gently. "Now you."

Frigid raised her hand, tears already welling in her eyes. She pressed her palm beside Kimiko's, their hands side by side upon the stone.

The elemental rumbled a sound not of anger, but of recognition. A pulse of amber light glowed beneath its surface. The presence of the Gatekeeper, an off-worlder who listened, and an Icelandian who wept for it... it understood now.

It was remembered.

Frigid smiled, her tears finally spilling over. "You were never forgotten... not truly."

The elemental knelt fully, its head bowing low. A deep hum filled the chamber like a hymn sung by the mountain itself.

Stone light flowed from its body to theirs, and then into the ground, as though rooting a tree deep into the crust of the world. The amber glow dimmed. The tremors ceased.

And the elemental fell back into slumber.

The chamber went still.

Kimiko collapsed into Frigid's arms, utterly spent. Her aura dimmed, the Gatekeeper silent for now.

Frigid brushed hair from her friend's damp face. "You did it."

Kimiko nodded slowly, her eyes red. "We did it."

Above them, the stone sighed. And for the first time in millennia, the weight of ages lifted.

The Quiet Before the Wind

The skies above Sommara had cleared. For the first time in days, the sun broke through the pale clouds, casting golden shafts of light across the rocky terrain and illuminating the scars left by the elemental conflict. Stone fragments lay scattered across the ground, remnants of shattered golems, now little more than inert rubble. Birds returned to the cliffs, cautious but singing. The breeze, though still cool, carried with it the scent of salt and distant greenery.

The diplomatic vessel, battered but intact, had returned to its coastal landing site. A small encampment had been constructed from salvaged supplies and reinforced with elemental wards. For now, the team and their Icelandian allies have a rare reprieve.

Kimiko sat alone on a rock ledge overlooking the ocean, her knees drawn up to her chest. The Frostheart charm at her neck glowed faintly, steady but low. Her hair whipped gently in the wind, and her expression was unreadable. Within her, the Gatekeeper stirred faintly – silent since the confrontation with the stone elemental, but present.

The emotions of the elemental still clung to her. Weight. Shame. Immobility. Kimiko could feel how the stone had mourned its own existence, longing to serve, yet imprisoned in its own form. The despair had been different from the fire elemental's rage – colder, quieter. It had seeped into her bones.

She exhaled slowly.

Behind her, Frigid approached, her steps soft over the grass-lined stone. She said nothing at first, only sat beside Kimiko, allowing the silence to stretch.

"He wasn't cruel," Kimiko said eventually. "He was old. Tired. So tired. He just wanted to stop holding everything up."

Frigid nodded. "The elemental?"

"Yes. His burden was to hold together the roots of the world. He thought if he let go, maybe the others would be free too. Or... maybe they would crumble like he did."

Frigid looked out to the sea. "You felt all of that?"

Kimiko nodded. "I feel everything. Not just what they say or do. What they are. Their essence. The Gatekeeper doesn't just bring balance. He absorbs imbalance. Even when I rest, I don't feel rested. It's like I carry the weight of a thousand lives that never asked for mine to join them."

Frigid's gaze softened. "And yet you're still here."

Kimiko glanced sideways at her. "I don't know how."

Frigid placed a hand gently on Kimiko's shoulder and wrapping her wing to touch the other shoulder softly. It was a rare gesture, one not easily given by the would-be Queen. "Because you're strong. Stronger than anyone I've ever met. Even when you're breaking, you're protecting everyone else first."

Kimiko's jaw tightened. Her voice dropped to a whisper. "I'm not strong. I'm just hiding it better than most."

"Maybe," Frigid said. "But I also think the Gatekeeper chose you because you already understood what it means to put others above yourself. You don't need to become something else. You already are what he needed."

Kimiko looked down at the charm again. The heartbeat had stabilized. Quiet. Not gone.

"Thank you," she said.

Frigid stood and extended a hand. "Come on. We need to brief the others and prepare the ship. Freija's overseeing repairs. She's getting restless without something to punch."

Kimiko allowed herself a small smile and took her hand.

Back at the encampment, Freija was overseeing the loading of supplies and checking their next navigational coordinates. She turned as they approached.

"Finally. You two have your little heart-to-heart?"

"You were eavesdropping," Kimiko said, arching an eyebrow.

"Me? Never. I'm far too dignified."

Frigid rolled her eyes. "Ship ready?"

"Mostly. A few of the external wings need re-enchanting, but the engines are good. Our next stop is Dorland, the Southern Continent. The coastal Parliament outpost there has reported violent winds leveling whole forest sectors."

"The wind elemental," Kimiko said quietly.

Freija nodded. "Yeah. And this one's going to be different. The winds don't burn or crush. They scatter. Divide."

Kimiko looked to the horizon, where distant clouds had begun to form, gathering in slow spirals.

"Then we'll have to hold fast."

As the team reassembled and the vessel began to hum once more with magical energy, a single gust of wind rose from the east – gentle at first but growing. It whistled through the trees and over the rocks, curling around Kimiko like a whisper of things to come.

The wind was awakening.

And soon, they would have to face it.

The Whispering Sky

The skies above Dorland bore little resemblance to the crystalline clarity of Frostholm. Thick, roiling clouds churned like a living sea overhead, bruised with hues of slate and silver. As the diplomatic transport vessel crossed into southern airspace, turbulence rocked its reinforced hull, jostling the passengers inside with increasing force.

Kimiko sat in her harnessed seat near the command deck, eyes half-closed, one hand resting over her Frostheart pendant. The charm pulsed erratically, warning of unseen forces ahead. Her body hummed with residual power from the Gatekeeper, but this sensation was different – twisting, invasive. The winds weren't just wild.

They were aware.

The deck lights flickered. A violent cross-current slammed into the ship's starboard side, throwing several crew members into the walls. Freija shouted, catching one young ensign before she collided with a bulkhead. Frigid gripped the support rail with both hands, her wings flattened tightly against her back.

On the bridge, Captain Terina struggled with the controls, knuckles white as she barked commands. "Stabilizers are at seventy percent. Diverting energy to the forward thrusters!"

"It's not working," one of the co-pilots yelled. "We're getting pushed off course!"

Kimiko unbuckled and braced herself as she approached the cockpit. Her eyes were glowing faintly now, the Gatekeeper stirring within.

"Captain," Kimiko said, her voice low but urgent. "The wind knows I'm here. It's trying to tear us apart."

Terina looked at her, stunned. "What do you mean?"

"The elemental. It senses the Gatekeeper inside me. It's calling the storm to strike us. You need to get the others out of here. Let them take to the skies. We'll be its focus. The ship will draw its fury."

The captain cursed under her breath, then nodded sharply. She turned to the crew. "All non-essential personnel, abandon ship! Engage aerial extraction protocol. Frigid, Freija – get your people out. This craft is no longer a safe haven."

Freija stared at Kimiko, wings already half-spread. "What about you?"

"I stay with the ship," Kimiko said. "The Gatekeeper must remain contained. If I leave, it may spread the storm wider."

Frigid stepped forward. "You'll be alone."

Kimiko's voice was quiet. "I'm never alone. Not anymore."

Reluctantly, Frigid turned. "Everyone – flight formation Gamma. Ascend above the cloud wall. We regroup once we locate a safe descent path."

The side hatches opened with a hydraulic hiss. A rush of icy wind blasted through the hold. One by one, the Icelandian warriors launched into the sky, buffeted by gale-force winds but kept aloft by sheer determination and skill. Freija was the last to leap, her wings snapping wide as she soared into the clouds.

Inside the ship, Kimiko took the co-pilot's chair beside Terina.

"Strap in," the captain growled. "We're going in hard."

The Sight from Above

Above, Frigid and Freija fought for control in the violent air currents. The wind tore at their wings and armor, spinning several of the younger warriors off-course. Freija twisted through the chaos with expert precision, diving and climbing, grabbing an off-balance soldier and hurling them back into proper formation.

"Keep altitude!" Freija called. "Don't let the downdrafts pull you under!"

But even she was struggling. The storm was not natural – it shifted too quickly, blew from multiple directions at once, and carried a low, thrumming pressure that made her ears ring.

As they flew, the transport craft below dipped lower, its engines straining, the tail end sheared by a crosswind. With a final shudder, the vessel vanished into a canyon gorge framed by towering stone columns. A blast of wind roared after it.

Then, suddenly, the sky went still.

"Why did it stop?" a warrior asked.

Freija hovered in place, breathing hard. "Because it has what it wants."

Frigid's face turned pale. "It has Kimiko."

Conquering the Vortex

The wreckage of the diplomatic transport lay nestled against a jagged hill of broken shale and frost-bitten trees. Its hull was scorched in places, its undercarriage twisted where the crash landing had dragged it through the rocky terrain. Despite the damage, the vessel had held together well enough to protect its passengers.

Kimiko stepped down from the loading ramp, her eyes scanning the alien landscape of Dorland. Unlike the frost-covered peaks of Icelandia's northern lands, the southern terrain was marked by towering rock formations, twisting wind-carved pillars, and canyons that sang with an eerie, ever-present breeze. The air here felt thinner, tighter – as if the sky itself were listening.

Captain Terina stood beside her, already unfastening the outer hull panels. "The ship will need a full cycle of repairs. We lost stabilizers, a starboard aileron, and some of the comms relay. I'll stay with her. You should go."

Kimiko nodded. "I'll find the others."

Freija landed nearby, her wings folding tightly behind her back. The sky had cleared somewhat since the landing, though streaks of high cirrus clouds moved unnaturally fast. She stepped beside Kimiko, glancing toward the range of distant hills. "The rendezvous point is five klicks southeast. It'll take us a couple of hours on foot. You up for it?"

Kimiko adjusted the straps of her weapons pack. "I am. Let's move."

The two set off, descending into a narrow ravine blanketed by wind-swept dust and cracked stone. The path wasn't easy. The winds that hadn't let go of the ship still prowled along the higher cliffs, occasionally diving into the canyons in twisting, howling gusts. They passed broken trees bent sideways by the pressure and rock arches worn into strange shapes.

155

Halfway through the second hour, Freija raised a hand. "Hold."

Kimiko froze.

Across the ridge, perhaps thirty meters away, a swirling column of wind began to take shape. Dust and pebbles rose into the air, gathering mass and form until the twisting cyclone formed a vaguely humanoid figure. Arms and a head took shape, though translucent and always shifting. Where its eyes should have been, there were only twin streaks of pale light.

"Air golem," Freija whispered. "It's searching."

Kimiko pressed herself into the shadow of a rocky crevice. Freija did the same, using a natural dip in the cliff wall. The wind creature turned slightly, drifting along the canyon ledge. It moved silently despite the wind that composed it.

Kimiko could feel the pulse of the Gatekeeper within her. It was steady – watchful. A warning, not an urge to fight. She exhaled slowly and focused on remaining still.

The golem hovered for a moment, its head tilting as if listening to some ancient, silent command. Then it drifted on, vanishing into the valley beyond.

"It's hunting me," Kimiko said softly.

Freija nodded. "It knows the Gatekeeper is close. But not exactly where. Let's not give it a reason to get curious."

They moved more cautiously after that, keeping low to the terrain and avoiding the open ridgelines. Eventually, they emerged onto a flatter plain that opened to a small camp nestled at the base of a wide, upturned cliff. The winged figures of several Icelandian warriors could be seen resting or sharpening weapons.

Frigid approached the group, speaking with a new arrival.

He was a tall man – almost five-foot-seven – with deep azure skin and a cloak of wind-silk fluttering behind him. His wings were broader than most, and his hair was woven into intricate braids, a sign of southern nobility.

"You made it," Frigid said with visible relief as Kimiko and Freija approached.

"Barely," Freija replied. "Storms tried to knock us out of the sky. We lost the ship. Kimiko and I hiked the rest."

VAEL

The southern warrior stepped forward. "I am Commander Vael of the Windspire Clan. Welcome to the Tempest Plains. You're lucky to have survived."

Kimiko bowed slightly. "We were guided by purpose."

Vael nodded. "Then you must be here for the mountain."

He pointed eastward, toward a range shrouded in a spiraling mass of clouds that refused to move. Unlike the rest of the sky, which changed with the wind, this formation remained locked in place like a great vortex coiled around a peak.

"That," he said grimly, "is Mount Caeloras. The winds have grown worse with every passing cycle. Entire villages have been pulled apart. Our best scouts say something ancient slumbers in the eye of that storm."

Freija folded her arms. "Let me guess. You think it's your elemental."

Vael's expression turned serious. "We know it is. And it's growing restless."

Kimiko felt the Gatekeeper stir inside her again – not with fear, but anticipation.

Another storm was coming.

And they would have to face it head-on.

The Wind that Resists

The clouds above Dorland swirled in uneven spirals, creating towering walls of vapor that continuously shifted shape. Lightning danced occasionally between them, but without thunder – silent, ominous, unpredictable. At the base of the towering mountain that locals called Mount Caeloras, the wind howled in constant, bitter gusts. The landscape was rocky and uneven, scattered with jutting stones and wind-worn trees bent from decades of constant gales.

Frigid, Kimiko, Freija, and the rest of the Icelandian warriors approached from the south. Kimiko's cloak billowed wildly behind her as she crouched near a rocky ledge, peering ahead.

Small wind golems – twisting humanoid cyclones roughly the size of a eight-foot humanoid – patrolled in shifting patterns near the lower cliffs of the mountain. Each one moved with eerie silence, their forms flickering like dancing tornadoes. Their feet never truly touched the ground, swirling instead just above it, and their arms flared occasionally with sharp, compressed blasts of air.

Frigid crept up beside Vael, "Have you fought any of those things?"

Vael nodded grimly. "Yes. Dozens. But blades, arrows, even energy bolts pass right through them. Like slashing at fog."

Freija scanned the field. "Then charging them outright is suicide."

One of the Icelandian warriors, a young fighter named Sorn, tilted his head. "They're self-contained."

Frigid turned toward him. "What!?! What do you mean?"

Sorn pointed. "They don't affect the air around them. Their vortex is internal – tight, controlled, except when they shoot those funnel blasts from what I guess you could call hands."

Kimiko narrowed her eyes. "Meaning if we don't enter their funnel paths, they won't knock us down."

Sorn nodded again. "If we could only slow them down..."

"Say that again, warrior," Freija said, her eyes narrowing.

"If we could only slow them down," Sorn repeated, more firmly.

Vael stroked his chin, his pale white hair dancing in the gusts. "Slow them down... yes. Salt. Sand. Small pebbles. That might work. Add friction to the vortex, increase the drag. They'd lose cohesion."

Frigid blinked. "Weigh them down?"

"Precisely," Vael said. "Disrupt the centrifugal force. Wind cannot cut through clutter – it needs flow. Debris interrupts that. Causes resistance."

Freija's face lit with purpose. "We test it. Now."

She pointed to three nearby warriors. "You three – grab bags, scoops, anything. Gather all the sand, pebbles, and grit you can find. Fast. Make sure to keep it small."

The warriors sprang into action. One filled a large cloth sack with crushed rock and hardened soil. Another dragged a half-collapsed barrel out of a supply pack and began shoveling sand into it.

Freija then stepped out from behind the rocks and shouted toward the nearest golem. "Hey! Windbag!"

The golem heard her. It turned instantly and surged toward her, spiraling at great speed. Its arm raised, and a focused stream of compressed air shot from its palm like a cannon. Freija rolled under the blast and took to the skies, wings snapping open in a powerful gust.

As the golem passed below, the three warriors soared overhead, each releasing their payloads of sand and grit. The debris rained down directly into the swirling mass.

The result was immediate.

The golem's vortex began to sputter, its form breaking apart into smaller strands of wind. Its figure stumbled – then slowed – then lost cohesion entirely. With a final whirling gasp, it dissolved into harmless mist.

"It worked!" one of the warriors shouted.

Frigid waved her spear. "Into four-man teams! One bait, three overhead with debris! Don't engage unless you have the drop!"

Dozens of Icelandians sprang into action. Throughout the canyon base, bait warriors flew in low patterns, taunting the golems into pursuit.

When the creatures surged after them, teams above dumped pouches of coarse sand, pebbles, or shattered rock. One by one, the golems faltered – some slower than others, but all showing weakness.

One squad overloaded a golem with a blast of powdered crystal. The golem shrieked in a high-pitched howl before imploding into a glittering cloud. Another was taken down with three separate sand drops from different angles.

Freija landed beside Kimiko, brushing dust from her shoulders. "We're learning. Fast."

Kimiko nodded, though her eyes remained focused on the peak above them. "But this is just the edge of it."

Vael approached, dropping his bag of sand. "You'll be climbing that," he said, motioning toward the towering cliffs.

Kimiko's eyes followed the impossible height. Wind spiraled up its length like an invisible snake. "Of course I am."

Vael pulled two climbing harnesses from his pack – both well-used but sturdy. "Figured you'd need one. No wings."

Kimiko took the harness with a nod. "Thank you."

Vael turned to Freija. "And this one is for you."

Freija blinked. "Me?"

"You'll climb beside her. That mountain's winds will try to rip anyone from the sky. You're fast, but this isn't about speed. It's about being there if she needs you."

Freija accepted the harness slowly, glancing at Kimiko. "Understood."

Frigid stepped up. "We'll climb from the east side. The winds are weaker in the early morning, and the shadows will give some cover. I'll stay with Vael and the others and monitor from above. We'll be your eyes."

Vael nodded in agreement. "Then we make final preparations tonight. We move at dawn."

The team took a long breath beneath the swirling sky. The mountain loomed tall and unyielding.

The battle for balance was far from over – but at least now, they had a way to fight the wind.

And tomorrow, they would begin the climb.

The Climb

The sky was still a deep violet hue as dawn broke over Dorland. Faint streaks of morning light bled through the swirling cloud cover above Mount Caeloras. Winds shrieked across the rocky ridges, tearing through the cracks and hollows like whispered warnings.

At the base of the towering mountain, Kimiko knelt in silence, adjusting the straps of her harness while checking the weight and balance of her climbing gear, ropes, and carabiners. She looked up the cliff face as it disappeared into mist and motion. The wind howled constantly, but she remained unmoved.

Freija walked over, her own harness half-fastened and her wings folded tight against her back. She looked at Kimiko with a raised brow. "So, be honest… do you have any climbing experience?"

Kimiko glanced sideways – and then, in a moment of rare levity, burst into laughter. Not a chuckle. A full, body-shaking laugh that echoed against the stone and momentarily drowned out the wind.

Freija blinked, caught off guard. "Was that… funny?"

"You do know I'm a trained ninja and assassin, right?" Kimiko smirked, her voice warm despite the cold.

Freija smiled. "Okay, yes, but I'm not from Earth. You still haven't explained what a 'ninja' even is. Sounds like a small animal that hides in trees."

Kimiko shook her head. "It means that climbing – without a harness, in pitch darkness, over sharp rocks, in bad weather, while someone is trying to kill you – is second nature to me. But today I have proper gear and I can see what I am doing."

"Great," Freija muttered, tightening her belt. "Remind me to never get on your bad side."

The pair approached the base of the ascent. Above them, the wind howled with new fury. Visibility dropped dramatically as thick fog poured down the cliff like a slow avalanche.

A horn sounded behind them. Frigid and several Icelandian warriors, including Vael, took to the air in formation, wings flaring wide against the current.

"They're going up fast," Freija said, shading her eyes. "Let's go."

They began to climb. Kimiko instructing Freija on proper use of gear and securing a carabiner before pulling up the ropes from below.

The stone was slick and jagged, carved from ancient volcanic rock that had been shaped by centuries of wind erosion. Every handhold had sharp edges. Every foothold could crumble at a moment's notice.

The wind battered them in violent gusts, nearly lifting them from the surface. Kimiko led the way, moving like water – flowing between cracks, pressing close to the stone, unfazed by the gale. Her breathing remained steady, her movements fluid.

Freija, on the other hand, struggled.

Despite her strength and her agility in the air, climbing was not something she had trained much for. Her gloves slipped more than once, and her boots lost grip twice in the first hundred feet.

About halfway up, the wind surged with a banshee shriek. Freija slipped again – this time completely losing her grip. Her body whipped away from the cliffside with a cry, her safety line keeping her from falling too far.

"Freija!" Kimiko shouted, anchoring herself and holding the line tight.

Freija's wings shot open. The wind caught her, nearly throwing her higher, but she angled herself, flaring the feathers just right to slow her fall. She twisted and kicked off the rock, slamming back into the cliff face and grabbing a lower hold.

She dangled there for a moment, chest heaving.

"Still alive?" Kimiko asked, her voice firm but gentle.

"Barely," Freija muttered. "Stars above, I hate this."

"You're doing fine." Kimiko anchored herself again and reached down. "Just focus. You've flown through artillery fire. This is just vertical walking."

"Vertical walking with death below me. Not the same."

"Still impressive." Kimiko gave a small grin. "Now come on."

With Kimiko's guidance and steadying encouragement, Freija regained her momentum. They pressed upward, higher into the mist.

Above them, Frigid and Vael fought the wind's fury. Kimiko looked up just in time to see the air shift violently, curling around the airborne warriors like a living serpent.

The gusts intensified. One by one, the flyers were thrown off course, their formations breaking apart. Frigid spun to regain control, her voice faint in the wind.

"North side! Fly around to the north side!" Frigid cried.

With effort, the winged warriors banked away from the cliff face, vanishing into the cloud cover.

Kimiko turned to Freija, her expression hardening. "It's just us now."

Freija gritted her teeth. "Then let's finish it."

They continued.

The last segment of the climb was the steepest – an almost vertical wall of black stone veined with shimmering quartz. The wind funneled here like it was alive, striking in jarring, unpredictable bursts. A few times, Kimiko had to flatten against the rock and brace herself just to avoid being thrown backward.

Finally, after what felt like hours, Kimiko's hand found the edge of a narrow ledge carved into the cliff.

She pulled herself up and collapsed onto the stone platform, chest heaving, limbs trembling from tension – not fatigue.

Seconds later, Freija clambered over the edge and dropped beside her. She rolled onto her back and stared at the grey sky above.

"That," she panted, "was horrifying."

Kimiko exhaled and pulled her hood tighter. "You did well."

"I slipped three times."

"And caught yourself all three. That's success where I come from."

Freija sat up slowly. Around them, the fog swirled in thick curtains, revealing little beyond the stone beneath their boots. The platform stretched forward into the side of the mountain. Somewhere, just beyond the mist, was the next entrance.

Kimiko stood, her body taut with tension. The Frostheart charm at her neck pulsed faintly, echoing her heartbeat.

"They're not here yet," Freija said, scanning the mist for signs of Frigid or the others.

"They'll make it." Kimiko stepped toward the cavern entrance. "But for now, it's just us."

And in the distance, beyond the veil of clouds, something stirred in the wind – watching. Waiting.

The Eye of the Storm

The temple within Mount Caeloras was unlike anything Kimiko or Freija had ever seen.

Carved into the mountain itself, it was a place suspended between the sacred and the forgotten. No lanterns lit their way, yet the air shimmered with pale silver light that pulsed faintly through the marble-veined stone, as though the walls themselves breathed. The wind outside continued to howl, pressing against the temple with an urgency that rattled the frost-slick columns and echoed through the great halls like a restless spirit.

Kimiko stepped lightly over a cracked stone threshold, her senses heightened. Every step she took caused the wind to stir, almost as if the structure was responding to her presence. The whorled carvings on the walls – spirals, arcs, feathered motifs – seemed to ripple with movement, even in the dim light.

"This place... it's alive," Freija murmured beside her, wings furled tightly and ice swords in hand. She touched one of the swirling carvings and drew her hand back in surprise. "It's warm."

Kimiko nodded. "It's responding to us."

The deeper they moved into the temple, the louder the wind grew – but not with ferocity. It whispered. It spoke in fragments. Echoes. Emotions. Warnings.

A low hum traveled through the floor beneath their boots. The walls occasionally moaned like old ice, and with every gust that tunneled through the archways, came images – flashes of memory not their own.

An Icelandian village destroyed by sudden storm. A frozen mountain shattered by sonic wind. A young Icelandian girl weeping into the gale as her family vanished into the sky.

Freija paused near a vast mural. It depicted a winged figure – tall, imposing, and cloaked in swirling air. Below it were dozens of smaller figures bowing in reverence. "The Wind Elemental," she whispered. "But… it's not a monster. It's…"

"Worshipped," Kimiko finished, eyes tracing the spiraling lines that encircled the mural.

Just then, the wind shifted.

Without warning, a vortex erupted from the corridor behind them, roaring like a tornado unleashed. The pull was instant – powerful. Freija was closest, and the current yanked her backward off her feet.

"Freija!" Kimiko shouted, springing into action.

Freija's wings snapped open in reflex, but the air inside the temple turned against her, flipping her sideways and slamming her into a pillar. She tumbled through the air toward a swirling pit that had suddenly cracked open in the floor – dark, spiraling, endless.

Kimiko leapt.

She twisted midair and caught Freija's arm, slamming her other hand into a jagged groove in the wall. Her muscles screamed as the wind tried to drag them both into the abyss. Freija, dazed and winded, clung to Kimiko as tightly as she could.

"I've got you!" Kimiko shouted.

"I hate climbing!" Freija gasped back.

With a final grunt of effort, Kimiko pulled them both clear of the vortex. The pit sealed itself immediately afterward, like the wind had blinked.

The gusts calmed – but the temple felt colder. The whispering voices had returned, louder now. More desperate.

Kimiko helped Freija to her feet. Her Frostheart charm pulsed faster than ever.

"They're not trying to kill us," Kimiko said quietly. "They're trying to show us something."

Freija, still catching her breath, looked up. "That thing nearly *ate* me."

Kimiko pointed to the next mural – one that showed the same elemental figure in chains, bound by flowing ribbons and storm-clouds.

Its face was obscured, but the posture was unmistakable: Agony. Isolation. Betrayal.

"She's not just a force of nature," Kimiko said. "She was a guardian. Like the Gatekeeper. But she was left here. Alone."

The voices in the wind grew mournful. Images of collapsing temples. Battles between elementals. The sealing of the Wind Elemental deep inside the mountain as her shriek of rage echoed across the sky.

"It wasn't just imprisonment," Kimiko whispered. "It was exile."

Freija approached one of the carvings – a handprint, large and surrounded by spiraling runes. "Maybe she fought the others. Maybe she lost control."

Kimiko stepped closer. "Or maybe she was *too powerful* – so they feared her."

Then, a flash.

A blinding burst of light erupted from the far side of the chamber. A concussive gust knocked both women backward. Kimiko hit the ground and rolled; Freija was blown into a low wall, momentarily stunned.

When the wind settled, the chamber had changed.

A swirling column of air rose between them, like a barrier of spinning mist. It howled with a different tone now – not rage, but *desperation*.

Kimiko stood, shielding her eyes. "Freija!"

"I'm alright!" Freija called back. "But I can't get to you!"

The voices in the wind rose again, surrounding Kimiko alone now. *You are the Vessel. You are the balance. Why have you come?*

Kimiko's heart pounded. She looked toward the barrier, where the shape of a towering figure was forming – broad, faceless, yet unmistakably *aware*.

The Wind Elemental had found her.

And it was ready to speak.

The Divide

Kimiko – The Hall of Air and Silence

Kimiko awoke not with a start, but with a drifting sensation – as if her body were weightless, suspended in a dream without gravity.

Around her, there was no floor, no ceiling. The space was a vast hall of sky, painted in shades of white and silver, with ribbons of soft light that curved and twisted through the air like wind given form. Bits of debris floated around her – shards of ice, crumbled stone, even leaves long faded to ash. Everything hovered.

She breathed, but there was no sound – only silence so deep it throbbed.

Where am I? she wondered.

"Within her," came the Gatekeeper's voice – distant, strained. *"Within the heart of the wind. Be cautious. Air is… difficult for us."*

Kimiko turned slowly, adjusting her balance without even thinking – letting her instincts guide her as she rotated in weightless space. Her hands brushed a floating doorframe made of mist. It dissolved into sparkling particles.

Then, the vision began.

The Wind Elemental's memory wrapped around her like a storm cloud.

A tall Icelandian woman stood atop the highest peak of the Western Sky Cliffs – long before the continents were united. She wore robes of white and gold, wings vast and unfurled, eyes burning with silver flame. Around her were hundreds of followers, kneeling in reverence.

"She was their protector," the Gatekeeper murmured. *"The wind was hers to command, not for destruction – but for flight, for breath, for voice."*

The memory twisted. War came. A storm of imbalance. The other elementals rose, corrupted by emotion – flame's rage, stone's pride, ice's fear.

The Wind Elemental fought to maintain harmony. She tried to unite the skies and the land. But they turned on her.

She was too unpredictable, too free. So they bound her.

Kimiko watched as the proud woman was shackled with runes carved into the air, forced into the mountain temple, her wings clipped by betrayal. Her voice, once a song of the skies, became a howl of torment.

Freedom turned to captivity.

Kimiko felt something stir in her chest.

She knew this feeling.

Her whole life had been dictated by silent obedience. Loyalty. Discipline. Never vulnerability. Never truth. The life of a shadow, a weapon – never her own.

"She was like me," Kimiko whispered. *"They took her purpose and called it danger. They took her freedom and called it peace."*

The Gatekeeper's voice was quieter now. *"She is not evil. But she is broken. Just as you once were. Help her remember who she was. Before the storm."*

Freija – The Temple Below

Freija grunted as another gust of wind slammed against the carved pillar she hid behind. Her wings were tucked in tight. The wind had teeth.

At the far end of the chamber, the swirling vortex still separated her from Kimiko, who was now completely out of sight – swallowed into the heart of the storm.

She pressed her palm to activate her comms. "Frigid? Vael? Do you read?"

A moment of static, and then Frigid's voice crackled through. "We see the storm. It's localized around your position. Are you safe?"

"Define 'safe,'" Freija muttered, peeking around the pillar. Three air golems floated just beyond the threshold, swirling upright on invisible feet, eyes glowing with pale light. "We've got company. But I'm holding."

"Don't engage alone," Vael's voice cut in. "We're circling the upper cliffs. Winds are chaotic, but we're finding paths through."

Freija smiled despite herself. "Tell them to fly smart."

She deactivated the comms and turned back toward the chamber. The golems didn't charge – but neither did they retreat. They hovered, waiting.

You can't trap air. You guide it.

The thought was sudden, unbidden. She remembered Kimiko's words from the night before. The elemental wasn't attacking – it was defending.

Reacting.

Her eyes narrowed. She studied the golems again. Their forms flickered erratically when close to the walls, as if the wind had no place to go – bouncing off stone, creating eddies and turbulence.

She darted out from cover, slashing the air in front of one golem – not to strike it, but to redirect its path. The creature swirled aside, disoriented by the manipulation of flow.

Freija pivoted, using her wings not to fly, but to create counter-currents – small flaps and bursts of wind that sent the golems into momentary imbalance in the confined space.

It worked.

They weren't machines. They were currents. And currents could be turned.

But the victory was fleeting.

The wall of wind surged again, rattling the entire chamber. Freija turned toward it, teeth gritted. "Come on, Kimiko... whatever you're doing in there, make it count."

Kimiko – Memory and Revelation

Kimiko floated before the essence of the Wind Elemental, now forming into a more distinct shape – a woman of whirling light and cloud, tall and regal, eyes hidden beneath a swirling helm of mist. Her mouth did not move, but her voice echoed through the chamber.

"You are not one of them. Not of the sky. Why have you come?"

Kimiko held her ground. "To restore the balance."

173

"Balance abandoned me. My voice was silenced. My skies stolen."

"You were betrayed," Kimiko said. "But that doesn't mean everything must be destroyed. You're not alone anymore."

The elemental's form wavered. Storms danced in her silhouette.

"They made me a weapon. They locked me away. They feared what could not be caged."

"I know that pain," Kimiko said softly. "I've lived it. Used. Honored – but never loved. Never asked who I wanted to be."

A silence passed. Then a single word echoed from the storm.

"Help."

Kimiko floated closer, lifting her hand. "Let me."

The Wind Elemental's essence surged, wrapping around Kimiko in a cyclone of emotion – anger, sorrow, hope. Kimiko didn't resist. She let herself feel it all.

The past. The pain. The purpose.

And in that storm, she found understanding.

Freija – At the Barrier

The wall of wind faltered.

Freija stood in the silence, staring into the now-parted mist as a figure slowly emerged – Kimiko, her hair wind-swept, her eyes glowing with silver light, the aura of the Gatekeeper faint but steady around her.

"Kimiko…" Freija breathed.

Kimiko stepped down from the misty platform. "She's listening now."

Freija's heart stilled. "You reached her?"

Kimiko nodded once. "Not as an enemy. As someone who's lived the storm."

Far above, the wind howled once more – louder, but no longer wild.

Not a scream.

A voice.

And it was ready to speak the truth.

Whisper of Wings

Descent from the Storm

The winds above Mount Caeloras had calmed. Where once a violent gale howled in protest, now only a reverent breeze danced between the broken stone pillars and mist-wrapped arches of the ancient mountain temple.

Kimiko stood at the threshold, eyes still glowing faintly from the Gatekeeper's touch, her body exhausted but upright. Freija stood beside her, wings twitching slightly from the tension of the battle just passed. The swirling vortex that had separated them was gone, leaving behind silence and stillness.

From above, wings cut the sky. Frigid descended first, followed closely by Vael and two of their Icelandian warriors. The instant Frigid touched down, her arms wrapped tightly around Freija in silent relief. Then she turned to Kimiko, hesitation giving way to fierce gratitude.

"You're alright," Frigid whispered.

"For now," Kimiko said. Her voice was soft. "She's listening. But she hasn't decided yet."

Vael stepped forward, eyes scanning Kimiko with reverent curiosity. "We felt the change. The wind no longer fights us. You did something... remarkable."

Kimiko looked toward the summit, now shrouded in gentle clouds. "She's not evil. She's grieving. Her duty was turned into a prison."

The moment stretched long, filled only by the faint whistle of air threading through the high crags.

Vael broke the silence. "Come. The others await below."

Kimiko hesitated, eyeing the steep descent. "Climbing down won't be easy."

Vael stepped forward, kneeling slightly. "Then don't climb. You flew here in spirit. Now let us fly you home. Freija, please hand me back that harness."

Freija quickly unstrapped the harness and handed it over to Vael. He strapped the harness on showing Kimiko how the two harnesses can be latched together.

Kimiko blinked, then slowly climbed onto his back, arms wrapping around his shoulders. Vael adjusted his stance, wings spreading wide, muscles tense with power.

Frigid and Freija took to the air beside him.

As they descended together through the thinning clouds, Kimiko rested her head lightly between Vael's shoulders. Below, the landscape opened into the familiar contours of their previous encampment.

The wind hummed around them – not hostile, not broken. Merely waiting.

Campfire and Clarity

By the time they returned to camp, the sun was lowering behind the cliffs, casting long golden rays across the tents and frost-dusted rocks. The Icelandian warriors had gathered, tending to their gear and watching the sky with anticipation.

A fire crackled at the center of the camp. Kimiko sat closest to it, the warmth grounding her, while Freija and Frigid rested on nearby stone stools. Vael paced a slow circle around the flame, speaking with the other senior warriors.

Kimiko lifted her gaze as the discussion quieted. "She was a guardian. Not a monster. She gave flight to the skies, breath to the trees. But they didn't understand her."

Vael knelt across from her. "We forgot what she was meant to be."

"She was betrayed," Kimiko said. "She was bound for being free."

Frigid looked into the fire, voice low. "And now she howls because no one listened."

"She's not alone anymore," Kimiko whispered.

Rituals of the Sky

As night deepened, Vael and the elders called a council among the warriors. Scrolls were unrolled, oral histories repeated, and old songs hummed into the flames.

One tale rose above the rest: the *Dance of Winds*.

"It was once performed at the highest peaks," an elder explained. "Not to command the air, but to honor it. To offer ourselves its rhythm. To remind the sky we are not its masters."

Frigid stood as the first volunteer. "Teach it to us. We'll do it tomorrow."

Freija groaned. "Is this going to involve synchronized wing work? I fly solo, remember?"

Frigid smirked. "You'll manage."

As they practiced the first few movements beneath the stars, Kimiko sat apart from the group. Her gaze was distant, but peaceful.

The Gatekeeper was quiet within her.

Not absent. Just listening.

Whispers in the Wind

Later that night, Kimiko lay beneath an open canopy, the stars above her flickering like ancient beacons. The wind moved around her like a lover's breath – curious, intimate, thoughtful.

Her eyes fluttered closed.

In her dreams, she saw a figure of wind and light, arms wide, wings unfurled.

"Soon," the Wind Elemental whispered.

Kimiko smiled in her sleep.

Tomorrow, they would dance.

Tomorrow, the storm would choose.

The Winds of Celebration

The camp at the base of Mount Caeloras had transformed by the following morning.

What was once a stark military outpost now flickered with colorful banners fashioned from old flight clothes, glowing lantern orbs, and aromatic clouds of spice-roasted root vegetables drifting over fire pits.

The Dorland warriors moved with a looseness that hadn't been seen in weeks – laughing, shouting in their wind-swept dialects, and preparing for the ritual known only as the *Dance of Winds.*

It was, according to Vael, a time-honored tradition after surviving a battle in the wind's domain. "We dance so the air knows we're not afraid," he had said. "And so our legs remember how to stand after flying through a hurricane."

Kimiko stood at the edge of the gathering circle, arms crossed, watching as two of the warriors tried to out-spin each other in midair while juggling thin silver ribbons. One failed spectacularly and crashed into a cook pot. Laughter erupted around him – even from the cook.

Vael appeared beside her, wiping his hands on a cloth and grinning. "I see you're observing instead of participating. Should I be offended?"

Kimiko raised a brow. "I was trying to figure out if that was dancing or a failed aerial combat maneuver."

"It's both," he boasted proudly. "You have to dance like the wind's watching but also like it's trying to knock you into a mountain."

Freija swooped down nearby, arms loaded with hot flatbread and two mugs of a fizzy, icy-blue drink. "Careful," she said, handing one to Kimiko. "This stuff is fermented root wine. Tastes like mint and regret."

Frigid arrived moments later, dressed not in armor, but in a flowing cloak that shimmered with ice-thread embroidery. She looked... relaxed. "For once, can we enjoy a celebration without you two turning it into a challenge?"

Freija looked deeply wounded. "You say that like it's a bad thing."

One of the local warriors struck a low, humming chord from a wind-harp – an instrument strung between two wooden wings that caught the wind and sang with its flow. More voices joined in, weaving a haunting but joyful melody through the air.

Vael stepped into the center of the circle and spun once, his white hair fluttering behind him. "This, outsiders, brothers, and sisters of frost, is where the Dance of Winds begins!"

Cheers erupted.

Another warrior tossed Vael a set of twin wind-blades – decorative, blunt-ended training weapons shaped like curved gusts. He twirled them dramatically and motioned to Kimiko. "Come on. You've danced with swords before, haven't you?"

"I was trained to eliminate people with swords," Kimiko said flatly.

"Then you'll fit right in," Vael winked, offering his hand.

Freija nudged her. "If you don't go out there, I swear I'll tell them about the time you sang karaoke that night after winning the war with Necra."

"You wouldn't." Kimiko said in defiance.

"Try me." Freija half-laughed.

With a resigned sigh and a slight smile, Kimiko took Vael's hand.

The dance was... not what she expected.

It wasn't structured or elegant. It was chaotic, spinning, dodging, leaping – sometimes in rhythm, often not. It mimicked flight, storm, and freedom. At one point, Vael deliberately fumbled a turn and spun directly into her. They both staggered and burst into laughter. She couldn't remember the last time she'd laughed that freely.

Freija joined next, gliding low and doing a dramatic, clumsy flip that ended with her flat on her back in the snow.

"Stick the landing, Princess!" someone yelled.

Frigid, ever the composed one, waited until a slow, graceful wind-harp solo began before entering the circle. Her movements were fluid, deliberate, and precise. A dancer of ice, not air. But when Kimiko reached out and spun her in a quick turn, Frigid didn't resist. She twirled and – almost – smiled.

The warriors clapped, shouted, and shared food and drink as the night wore on. The wind sang above them, not in fury, but in harmony.

Later, sitting around a low fire, Kimiko looked at the three warriors beside her – Frigid regal and strong, Freija wild and open-hearted, and Vael grinning with a blanket draped over his shoulders like a cape.

"I didn't think I'd find peace in a place like this," Kimiko said softly.

Vael raised his cup. "You didn't find it. You made it."

The fire crackled. The wind blew gently through the trees.

And for the first time since bonding with the Gatekeeper, Kimiko allowed herself to believe that the heart of a storm could also be a place of rest.

Return to the Ice

The soft morning light broke over the horizon in Dorland, painting the sky in hues of silver and gold. Dew clung to the grass and clung to the feathers of the Icelandian warriors still dozing around the dying embers of the fire from the night before. The celebration had faded into memory, leaving behind only the echo of laughter and the gentle lull of wind through the camp's trees.

Kimiko sat at the edge of the bluff, overlooking the ocean of clouds that separated them from the rest of Icelandia. Her legs were crossed, hands folded in her lap, and her eyes closed. Though her expression was calm, the Gatekeeper inside her whispered about shifting tides.

A presence was stirring in the north – colder, quieter, but far more patient than the others.

"Frost waits," the Gatekeeper said softly. "And it remembers."

Behind her, the rhythmic clanging of gear being loaded broke the stillness. The diplomatic transport sat nearby, its sleek hull shimmering in the dawn light. Engineers and crew moved with quiet urgency, reattaching auxiliary stabilizers and checking for structural damage sustained during the earlier crash.

Freija emerged from her tent half-armored, yawning as she buckled her belt. "I vote we never fight wind again. Or dance in it, for that matter."

"You weren't complaining when you were spinning like a snowflake last night," Frigid said, approaching with her long coat billowing behind her.

Freija smirked. "That's because I was winning."

Captain Terina stood by the boarding ramp, reviewing a crystal datapad as she conferred with her navigation officer. Her sharp silver eyes flicked up as the group approached. "Ship's ready. The flight path to the Frostholm is stable. The winds have calmed, but I recommend we take a less direct path around the eastern sea currents."

Frigid nodded, arms folded. "We need to return to Frostholm immediately. The King and Queen must be told everything."

"We also need to review the scrolls on the frost elemental again," Kimiko added, standing and brushing frost from her robes. "It's the final one. And it's waiting for us."

Vael joined them near the ship's base, a pack slung over his shoulder. "Don't suppose you need one more ice-savvy warrior for the road?"

Freija grinned. "Already miss us?"

"I just want to see where this ends," Vael replied with a grin. "And make sure you don't get yourselves killed."

Frigid glanced to Kimiko. "What do you think?"

Kimiko looked between the three of them, then gave a small nod. "He flies well. He fights well. And he hasn't insulted my cooking. He's in."

Vael mock-bowed. "High praise indeed."

Within the hour, the entire crew was aboard. Kimiko, Frigid, and Freija took their places in the forward observation chamber just behind the cockpit, while Captain Terina ran final checks.

Vael's transport ship was warming up its engines nearby with many of his troops preparing to board.

The engines rumbled to life, humming with arcane power. The vessel rose gracefully from the landing pad, scattering loose snow and dust into the trees as it gained altitude.

As Dorland shrank beneath them, Frigid sat with her arms resting on the curved railing, staring toward the distant northern peaks. Her voice was quiet. "We left it behind. But it was always going to end where it started."

Freija's eyes narrowed thoughtfully. "Do you think the frost elemental knows we're coming?"

Kimiko spoke without turning from the window. "It's ice. Ice doesn't rage like fire. It doesn't shake the earth or howl like the wind. It waits. It watches."

Frigid's hand instinctively moved to her Frostheart charm. "Then let's hope we're not too late."

The ship banked east, then turned north – toward the spires of Frostholm that pierced the clouds like frozen teeth.

Back to the ice.

Back to the beginning.

Frostholm Briefing

The icy gates of Frostholm parted with a low groan as the diplomatic transport descended into its reserved landing cradle. The vast fortress glistened with a fresh layer of frost, and the pale morning light refracted off the spires, casting ghostly silhouettes across the landing deck. Snowflakes danced gently in the air, stirred by the faint hum of the ship's engines powering down.

Kimiko, Frigid, and Freija descended the ramp side by side, cloaked against the chill. Their armor bore the marks of distant continents, and their eyes carried the weight of the battles they had survived. Winged guards saluted them with synchronized precision.

A high-ranking aide bowed low before them. "Welcome home, Lady Frigid. Lady Freija. Honored Vessel. His Majesty awaits your audience."

Frigid gave a curt nod. "Take us to him."

The halls of the palace felt colder than usual. As the trio was escorted through the long corridors of blue crystal and frost-etched stone, the walls whispered with a stillness that only came before great storms. Servants paused in their duties, watching with wide eyes as the three warriors passed.

The escort halted before the great double doors of the King's private chamber. With a formal gesture, the aide swung them open. Inside, King Frostran stood at the head of a long frostglass table, Queen Glaciana seated beside him.

The King looked older than he had just weeks ago. His regal bearing remained, but there was fatigue behind his eyes. Glaciana, composed and poised, gave a slight smile as her daughters entered.

"Frigid. Freija. Kimiko," she said warmly. "Please. Sit."

The three stepped forward. Frigid remained standing as she began. "We bring news from all three continents. The fire elemental was sealed beneath the Eastern caverns. The stone elemental subdued in the Western range. And the wind... honored in the skies above the Southern Continent."

Freija leaned forward. "Each one was more than a force of destruction. They were guardians, twisted by imbalance. But not beyond reason."

King Frostran folded his hands together. "And the golems? The attacks?"

"We discovered their weaknesses. Coordinated efforts allowed us to overcome them," Frigid explained. "But it wasn't easy. And they will return if the frost elemental awakens."

The Queen turned her gaze to Kimiko. Her voice was calm, but there was a quiet gravity behind her words. "And you? You have been silent. Tell us what the Gatekeeper has revealed."

Kimiko bowed her head respectfully. "Your Majesties, I can only offer what I understand through my bond. The Gatekeeper does not normally speak as we do. It shares through emotion, memory, and presence."

She looked up, her eyes catching the chamber's pale light. "The elementals were not created to destroy. They were meant to maintain harmony. Each one served as a protector of balance. But when fear, anger, and betrayal poisoned that balance, they were sealed away. Not with hate – but sorrow."

The King listened without interruption.

Kimiko continued. "Each elemental I've encountered feels older than time. They were left alone, confused, tormented by a world that forgot them. It is not power they seek – it is purpose."

Queen Glaciana sat back, her expression thoughtful.

Kimiko's voice softened. "In every battle, I felt their pain as if it were my own. And so did the Gatekeeper. He exists not to control them, but to remind them of their place in the natural order. To restore the symmetry that was lost."

The chamber fell silent.

Then, slowly, King Frostran rose. He approached the table, stopping across from Kimiko.

"When I first realized the Vessel not being one of Icelandia," he said, his voice measured, "I was skeptical. Resentful, even. I had spent my life believing it would be one of my daughters. That our bloodline bore the duty."

He studied her closely. "But I see now it is not blood alone. It is the spirit. The heart. The resolve."

Kimiko inclined her head. "Thank you, Your Majesty."

The King looked to Frigid and Freija, then back to Kimiko. "We have one left. And it is here, beneath our feet. The frost elemental stirs, and it knows what is coming."

Frigid stepped forward. "Then we must act before it awakens fully."

Frostran gave a single nod. "Rest tonight. Prepare. Tomorrow, we plan our final descent."

And with that, the chill in the room no longer felt like fear.

It felt like resolve.

Shattering Calm

The Awakening

The debrief in the King's chamber had been calm, orderly – until the floor shifted.

It was subtle at first, a strange, almost imperceptible vibration beneath their feet. Frigid paused mid-sentence, one hand braced on the obsidian table, brow furrowed. Freija, pacing near the frostglass window, looked up sharply.

Then the second tremor hit.

This time, it was unmistakable. The frostglass chandeliers above swayed violently. Books and scroll cases tumbled from shelves. The deep groan of moving earth echoed through the spires of Frostholm.

"A quake?" the Queen asked, rising.

"Not natural," Kimiko said, her voice tight. Her hand moved to the Frostheart charm at her neck, which pulsed erratically against her chest. "She's awake. The Frost Elemental. She senses us. She senses me."

Frigid dashed to the window. What she saw chilled her more than the shaking floor.

Avalanches. Massive ones. Entire cliffs shearing from the mountainside, rolling down in towering clouds of ice and stone, roaring toward the lower villages and outer districts of Frostholm.

"No," Frigid whispered. "It's happening now!"

The King stood, eyes wide. For a heartbeat, even he was stunned.

Then he moved.

"Sound the Frosthorn," he ordered, voice ironclad. "All elite warriors to the courtyard. We deploy immediately."

A court aide bolted from the room.

Freija turned to him. "We don't have time to plan. We act now, or Frostholm will be buried."

"Agreed," the King said, already striding toward the armory alcove behind his throne. "I will lead the rally myself."

Suddenly the frosthorn siren rang out calling all warriors to the courtyard.

The Frantic Realization

Kimiko gripped the edge of the frost-tempered table, her knuckles pale. The Gatekeeper inside her surged in warning – not in fear, but recognition. It was ancient. Familiar. Terrifying.

"This one isn't like the others," she murmured. "The fire burned, the stone crushed, the wind howled – but this... this is silence. She doesn't scream. She waits. Cold and calculating."

Freija turned to her. "What does she want?"

"Nothing," Kimiko said. "She sees us the way frost sees a tree. Something to bury. To preserve in stillness. Forever."

The Queen crossed to her daughters, her expression grim. "Then we must move. Before she does."

Frigid nodded. "Assemble the captains. Pull every frostlancer, flight mage, and windguard available. We need full formation strength."

"Already in motion," the King said, now donning his froststeel armor. The family crest shimmered on his chestplate. "Today, we fly."

The Rally

The Frosthorn echoed through the city like a banshee's cry, loud enough to wake the dead beneath the ice. All across the palace, spires lit up with signal runes. Warriors scrambled into formation.

Kimiko stood in the courtyard beneath the sky, now veiled in thick snow. Wind screamed between the towers. Above them, ice dragons carved into the architecture stared down in judgment.

Frigid and Freija donned their gear with lightning precision, joined by squadrons of elite Icelandian fighters. Each wore winged harnesses, long cloaks, and weaponry etched with glacial glyphs.

Vael descended with his Southern Continent troops that were still waiting on the transport ship, having flown ahead when the tremors started. His wind-cloak was heavy with sleet.

"Late to the dance," he said, offering a grim nod to Frigid. "But I brought a few steps."

"You're always welcome," Freija said.

The King appeared on the central dais, flanked by Parliament guards. His presence silenced the storm itself for a breath.

"We are under siege by no army," he called. "But by the very spirit of our world – a force we once thought buried. The Frost Elemental has risen. And she remembers us."

A murmur of fear.

"But she does not remember that we… " he raised his sword overhead, "…are Icelandians. The wind did not take us. The fire did not break us. The earth could not bury us. And the frost?"

He pointed to the looming northern peaks, where distant avalanches painted the sky white.

"The frost is our birthright. We were born of it. We will tame it."

Cheers rang out. Swords lifted. Wings unfurled.

Kimiko's Doubt

As the warriors lifted into the sky in tight flocks, Kimiko stood at the edge of the courtyard. Snow whipped past her face. The Gatekeeper inside her trembled.

"This one... she's different," she whispered. "She knows I'm here. And she hates me."

Frigid stepped beside her. "She doesn't hate you. She fears you. Because you are change. You are warmth."

Kimiko's jaw clenched. Her breath clouded the air.

Freija touched her arm. "We go now. She won't wait for us to be ready. We go. And we finish this."

Kimiko nodded slowly, then drew a katana.

And beneath the crumbling cliffs of the North, the frost stirred.

The final elemental had awoken. And it would not go quietly.

Fire Against the Frost

Clash of Ice and Desperation

The cliffs outside the northern reaches of Frostholm roared with ancient fury.

Snow surged down the crags like a living tide, slamming into the icy plateau below. A wave of cold wind swept across the battlefield as dozens of frost golems marched forward from the misty chasm that now yawned wide where solid ground had once stood. Each golem stood over eight feet tall, their forms chiseled from glacial ice and embedded with glowing blue runes that pulsed with cold energy. Their eyes burned with white fire, soulless and unwavering.

The Icelandian warriors met them head-on.

Frigid led the charge, her frost-etched double-bladed spear slicing through the wind as she launched into the air, her wings spread wide. She struck the nearest golem with a spinning slash – only for the weapon to glance harmlessly off its icy torso.

Freija dove in next, blades like silver flashes through the swirling snow. Her twin swords sparked with cold light as they bit into the golem's arm… and slid off without leaving a mark.

"They're not breaking!" she shouted, flaring her wings to avoid a crushing blow.

"Hold formation!" Frigid called, sweeping low. "Delay them! Push them back!"

The frontline warriors obeyed, surrounding the golems in staggered phalanxes, wings tucked for stability as they tried every combat maneuver they knew. Spears shattered. Ice bolts glanced off with little effect. Even rune-etched axes, passed down for generations, barely made the creatures slow.

"We can't hurt them!" someone screamed.

"Just hold them!" another shouted. "Keep them from breaching the line!"

The frost golems advanced in silence. No growls. No roars. Only the crunch of boots on snow, and the heavy thud of impact as one slammed its massive fist into a soldier's shield, launching him back ten feet into the drifts.

Vael soared in from above and sliced with a frost-tipped glaive. When it bounced harmlessly off a golem's skull, he snarled. "We need fire!"

Frigid turned toward him. "Fire?"

"Heat melts ice," he yelled. "Send runners back to the fortress! Bring every torch you can carry!"

Vael twisted midair and pointed to a small cluster of warriors caught on the back lines. "You twenty – move! Break into the blacksmith's forge, the kitchens – anywhere with flame!"

The runners didn't hesitate.

The Furnace Rush

Back in Frostholm, the stone halls echoed with bootfalls and shouted orders. Warriors burst into chambers and shattered wooden chairs, benches, and training dummies. Others tore down old banners and tapestries to use as makeshift torch wraps.

One group reached the mess hall. Tables were flipped. Iron pots spilled. Flames from cooking hearths were repurposed into hasty torches, sticks wrapped in cloth and dipped into bubbling oil.

In the old Parliament chamber, a trio of warriors dragged one of the council's ancient ceremonial standards down and splintered it over a frozen brazier. Another lit the torn end of a tunic, using a nearby candle.

"We don't have time to make them perfect!" a younger fighter shouted, his eyes wild. "Just get them burning!"

Some used broken chair legs, others used blades wrapped in wool. One soldier came sprinting with half a flaming tapestry clutched in both hands, smoke trailing behind.

"Back to the cliffs!" Vael's voice rang through the comm crystals. "Fly, now!"

Turning the Tide

The sky turned black with the wings of returning warriors.

They descended like a second wave – this time armed with flame.

Freija, mid-dodge, caught a blazing torch tossed from above. She spun midair and slammed it across the face of an oncoming golem. Where her swords had failed, the fire left a burn mark.

The golem paused. Cracked. Melted.

"IT WORKS!" she shouted. "MELT THEM!"

Warriors screamed war cries and dove in with renewed fury. Flames struck chests and limbs. Blue runes flickered and dimmed as chunks of ice sloughed away. Torches roared with light, clutched in gloved hands as Icelandian fighters hurled them like javelins into the advancing frost beasts.

Frigid slashed a golem's leg with her spear, then thrust a burning torch under its knee. The heat hissed and crackled, and the joint exploded in a puff of steam. The golem fell sideways, flailing.

"Take out their legs!" she screamed. "Drop them to the ground!"

Vael landed beside her, two firebrands in hand. He slammed both into the chest of a towering golem, then jumped back as it collapsed, hissing, into a pool of meltwater.

The warriors fought with desperation and clarity. One team of three worked in unison – two baiting a golem into raising its arms while the third soared down from above, driving twin torches into its shoulders. Another warrior tackled a golem into a crevasse, shoving a flaming brazier into its chest before flying free.

The air stank of smoke, steam, and sweat. But the line held.

The Silent Pull

Amid the battle, Kimiko stood frozen.

She had not moved since the frost golems emerged. The wind and snow whipped around her, yet she remained still at the edge of the battlefield, her eyes glowing faintly with a blue-white fire. The Frostheart charm at her neck pulsed rapidly – faster than a heartbeat.

Her arms hung limp at her sides. Sparks of light began to crackle across her skin.

Electricity, pure and brilliant, spiraled from her shoulders down her arms in soft arcs. Her body began to shimmer with the aura of the Gatekeeper. Her breath fogged and caught, her mind drifting.

She turned, trance-like, and began walking toward the cavern entrance.

Freija spotted her, just as she felled another golem. "Kimiko?"

But a gout of frost-blast from a nearby golem forced her back. She dove to the side, shielding herself.

"Kimiko, stop!" she shouted.

Kimiko didn't hear. Or perhaps... she wasn't the one listening anymore.

She stepped beyond the frontlines. Toward the source. Toward the final elemental.

And the ice didn't melt beneath her feet.

It parted.

The Last Threshold

The Descent into Frost

Kimiko stepped into the cavern alone.

The entrance yawned like the mouth of an ancient beast, lined with walls of jagged frost and a floor etched in layered hoarfrost. The air was deathly still. The moment she passed the threshold; silence pressed down on her like a frozen weight. Even the sounds of the distant battle – cries, fire, the breaking of ice – vanished.

Her body pulsed with the power of the Gatekeeper, electricity shimmering in arcs along her limbs. The Frostheart charm at her neck glowed so brightly it looked like a star carved from crystal, beating in rhythm with her heartbeat... and something else.

Deeper.

The cavern pulsed with ancient power.

Each step forward grew harder. Not because of the cold   it was more than that. A presence watched her, immense and old. It wasn't just the cavern that breathed. It was the frost itself.

"She's close," Kimiko whispered.

The Gatekeeper's voice echoed faintly within her mind. *"She was the first. The deepest. The one who chose stillness over destruction. Be cautious."*

And then, she was there.

The chamber opened like a cathedral of silence.

Massive ice columns stretched into shadow. At the center stood the Frost Elemental – a towering figure carved from ancient glacial ice, her body half-formed from mist and frost. Her face was regal but unreadable,

195

her eyes glowing with a cold, endless blue. There were no flames here, no sparks – only the eternal silence of ice that never melted.

Kimiko stepped forward. The Gatekeeper's energy rose within her, glowing across her limbs, casting blue-white light over the frozen walls.

"I am the Vessel of balance," Kimiko said softly. Then she began to speak in unison with the Gatekeeper. "I've come to bring harmony to the elemental forces. You are the last."

The Frost Elemental didn't move.

But the cold deepened.

A terrible silence followed. Then came the pressure.

Kimiko dropped to one knee, gasping. Ice formed instantly across her boots and legs. Her arms trembled as the Gatekeeper's power surged, trying to meet the Elemental's will. But this was not fire, nor stone, nor wind. This was age. Eternity.

"*You... challenge me?*" The voice wasn't words – it was vibration, emotion, like glaciers shifting under miles of snow. "*You come with borrowed power. You are heat. You are change.*"

Kimiko's breath misted with every gasp. "I come... to bring balance... not to erase you."

The elemental's form shimmered.

"You are not of the frost. You are not still. You do not understand."

The Gatekeeper responded in unison. "We are bound by duty. We ask not for obedience – but trust."

The frost deepened.

Then the pain began.

Kimiko's vision dimmed. She screamed as the elemental's power surged forward, pressing into her body like a tidal wave of memory and grief. The Gatekeeper faltered, its energy flaring chaotically.

Outside the cavern, Frigid and Freija broke through the defensive lines of melting frost golems. Vael flew behind them, guiding a squadron. Behind them, the King and Queen descended from the sky with wings of silver and authority.

"Where is she?" the King demanded.

"There!" Frigid pointed to the archway where blue-white light pulsed erratically.

Freija's heart dropped. "She's alone."

They rushed forward. Inside, they saw her – Kimiko, standing against the weight of an elemental force older than any kingdom. Her back arched, her hands trembled. The frost was creeping up her arms like chains of ice.

"Kimiko!" Freija called, taking a step forward.

Kimiko didn't turn. Her knees buckled, and she collapsed with a choked cry.

Freija lunged.

And this time, Kimiko didn't stop her.

Freija crashed to her knees beside her, grabbing Kimiko's trembling hand. The moment their skin met, a flood of emotion slammed into her like a glacier collapsing into the sea.

She cried out in agony yet not from pain alone, but from the staggering depth of it.

Millennia of silence. Of waiting. Of being forgotten.

Freija's scream joined Kimiko's, her eyes wide with tears as the sheer *weight* of the Frost Elemental's isolation, her betrayal, her sorrow, poured into her soul. The cold wasn't just cold anymore. It was memory. It was sacrifice. It was love, frozen in time.

"I can *feel* her," Freija gasped, clutching Kimiko's shoulder. "She was left behind... abandoned. No one ever came back..."

Kimiko shook her head weakly. "That's why... I must stay. I can't let her... fade alone..."

From behind them, Vael stepped forward. His wings drooped in reverence, silver feathers catching the frostlight like broken halos. His face, usually carved in command, was softened now... by grief and purpose.

He knelt behind Freija, pressing a hand to both her back and Kimiko's shoulder.

He yelled with from the overwhelming emotion and pain he was now sharing with them. He yelled in broken words, "She shouldn't carry it alone... Not this burden... not this honor."

The energy shifted.

Kimiko gasped as the agony dispersed, not erased, but spread thin, shared between them. The elemental's grief no longer drowned her. It resonated. Echoed.

From across the chamber, Frigid stood frozen in place, then took a sharp breath and ran.

She dropped beside Kimiko with a force that cracked the frost beneath her knees. Without hesitation, she seized Kimiko's other hand and laid her palm atop Freija's arm.

Her voice broke as her back arched and wings flared, "You always think it's you who must endure it all, Kimiko. But you're not alone. Not here. Not now. Not in *our* world."

Tears clung to her lashes and froze there like tiny icicles of defiance.

Around them, the elite guards of Icelandia moved – not by command, but by instinct. One by one, they stepped forward, removing gauntlets, laying bare hands on shoulders, arms, backs. It didn't matter who touched whom. The chain of honor was formed.

Then, the Queen stepped forward.

She lowered herself to her knees, shedding her fur cloak, and bowed her head before Kimiko and the Frost Elemental.

"I am Queen Glaciana," she said softly, reverently. "I speak for the throne. For the realm. For the ancient oaths made long ago and shamefully forgotten. But *you* remembered, Kimiko. You carried us here. You bore what we denied."

She laid a trembling hand atop Kimiko's heart. "We share your burden now."

A breath… an unseen wind… passed through the circle.

The Frost Elemental blinked for the first time.

And beyond the flickering stormlight stood the King.

He did not kneel.

He did not move.

But he bowed his head… not out of weakness, but profound respect.

The circle of warriors and royalty, of frost and flame, of past and present, knelt in frozen silence. Their eyes were closed. Their hearts open.

Kimiko's aura pulsed again, this time not in agony, but in harmony.

Stillness did not break.

It breathed.

A pulse of air swept through the chamber. Cold met current. Stillness trembled.

And the storm had only just begun.

Whisper of the Wind

They were all connected now, every warrior, every soul. From Queen Glaciana's trembling hand resting atop her daughter's shoulder, to Vael's palm pressed against Freija's back, to the glacial sentinels forming a ring around them – touching one another, grounding each other – they had become a single living conduit of memory, pain, and purpose.

At the center was Kimiko.

She knelt, eyes closed, her breath shallow but steady, engulfed in a shimmer of blue-white light. The Gatekeeper within her pulsed with a rhythm older than time, and through that pulse, the storm of the Frost Elemental had been absorbed not erased, but witnessed.

Kimiko's body swayed, and the circle swayed with her.

Freija's wings curled around the group like a protective shell. Frigid gritted her teeth, tears falling freely now, not from pain, but from fierce determination. Vael knelt, his body trembling, yet his hand never lifted. Queen Glaciana whispered prayers under her breath, her voice steady and sacred.

All of them shared the burden.

All of them bore witness.

And then the wind changed.

No sudden gust, no explosion of air. Just a soft stirring, like a sigh escaping the mountain's chest. The chamber, once pulsing with storm and light, grew eerily calm.

Mist curled downward from the vault's apex, delicate and slow. It shimmered with soft silver hues, like moonlight caught in smoke. From its folds emerged the form of a woman not made of flesh, but of air and motion, her outline flickering like wind-drawn silk.

The Wind Elemental had come.

She hovered, weightless, her expression a blend of sorrow and serenity. Her presence touched every cheek, every neck, every breath – her body *was* the air. She glided over the circle of joined warriors, her ethereal wings spiraling faint vortexes in her wake.

And she spoke not aloud, but into the bones of those present.

"You did not forget me."

Kimiko opened her eyes.

Her voice was hoarse, but resolute. "You were never forgotten. Just… buried."

A pause. Then, behind her, another voice answered.

It was the Frost Elemental. She shifted from the cavern's edge, her towering form now softened with understanding. "I buried you," she said bitterly. "Along with everything that made us whole."

"You buried pain," Wind replied, drifting closer to her ancient sister. "But so much more was lost with it."

A silence stretched between them… raw, ancient, aching.

Wind looked down at the joined circle of human and Icelandians. "They remembered for us."

Frost's glowing eyes turned to Kimiko. Then to Freija. Frigid. Vael. Glaciana. The circle of hearts and hands.

"And they shared it," Wind whispered. "Carried it. Chose to suffer what was not theirs."

The Frost Elemental bowed her head. Her limbs, once rigid and coiled with fury, loosened. "Then I… I will listen."

The chamber pulsed.

A ripple of wind and frost swept outward… not in violence, but in release. It passed through the circle like a sigh of forgiveness, leaving warmth in its wake. Ice melted at the seams. The blue of Kimiko's aura dimmed from blazing to steady glow.

The pain, though not erased, was finally balanced.

The Frost Elemental stepped back.

The Wind Elemental offered her hand.

And this time, the frost did not reject it.

Their fingers brushed – one of ice, one of air – and light burst between them, not with force but with *unity*. A soft shimmer expanded across the dome like a sunrise in fog. The wind ceased howling. The frost stopped trembling. The very atmosphere sighed in relief.

The balance was restored.

Kimiko's body gently sagged. Freija caught her, cradling her close. Frigid placed her forehead to Kimiko's, whispering something inaudible but full of love. Vael exhaled in exhaustion, and Glaciana pulled her arms tighter around the nearest soldier.

No one moved for a long time.

Then, slowly, the Wind Elemental turned. Her eyes, now gleaming with gratitude, settled on Kimiko.

"You remembered us."

"You *honored* us."

"And now, we remember you."

With a final gust of gentle air, she began to dissolve, drifting upward into the swirling silver mist. The Frost Elemental watched her go, then followed. Not in hostility, but in reverence.

When they were gone, only silence remained.

And in that silence, Kimiko whispered:

"It's done."

The Gatekeeper's light faded to a soft glow. The elemental chamber stilled.

And Icelandia… at least for now… was at peace.

Echoes in the Quiet

The air in Frostholm was still for the first time in days.

What had been wind, avalanche, and the shriek of ancient power had given way to silence – reverent, almost sacred. Above the city, the skies cleared, casting icy sunlight across spires etched in frostglass. Below, the people of the Northern Continent slowly emerged from their homes and strongholds, whispering thanks to the wind, the snow, and the heroes who had returned.

Inside the grand fortress, the King's private chambers were guarded like a vault.

Vael stood at the threshold, one hand on the hilt of his frost-split blade, the other braced across his chest in silent vigilance. When Frigid and Freija arrived – supporting Kimiko between them – he stepped aside wordlessly, his gaze never leaving the hall behind them.

Kimiko's steps were sluggish. Her body trembled from exhaustion. But the aura that surrounded her had not dimmed.

If anything, it glowed brighter now – an elegant storm of blue and white energy that shimmered faintly around her shoulders and neck. The Frostheart charm still beats like a second heart, pulsing with quiet power.

Inside the chamber, King Frostran and Queen Glaciana stood waiting.

The room was still, lit only by the soft flame of the central hearth. The air was warmer than usual, as if the lingering presence of fire and frost elementals had left a mark that even centuries of ice couldn't erase.

The King stepped forward slowly, concern etched into every line of his frost-hardened face. He motioned for Frigid and Freija to ease Kimiko into one of the high-backed chairs beside the fire.

The Queen sat beside her, brushing a strand of dark hair from Kimiko's forehead. "You've done it," she whispered. "The elementals... they've all been calmed. Icelandia is whole again."

Kimiko opened her eyes slowly, blinking against the warmth of the firelight. "It wasn't just me. I was the Vessel – but it was *us*. Freija, Frigid, the Gatekeeper... and all of them. The elementals didn't want destruction. They wanted to be remembered. To be free."

The King paced to the frostglass window and turned back, his voice low but firm. "Tell me the truth, Kimiko. Is it over? Is the Gatekeeper... gone?"

Kimiko hesitated. Then, slowly, she shook her head.

"No. He's still here. Still strong within me."

Her aura pulsed softly as she spoke.

"The bonding... was never meant to be undone. At least, not by Icelandian scrolls. The ancient texts were written for *your* bloodlines. For elemental heirs. But I'm not of this world. I carry a different kind of royalty. The scrolls said nothing about that."

The Queen looked startled. "You believe... the ritual can be reversed?"

"When I've recovered, yes," Kimiko said. "The Gatekeeper agrees. The bond can be released. But it will take time. Energy. Precision. And I have to be ready. Right now, he's... still holding too much of them within me."

Freija folded her arms, stepping forward. "Is it hurting you?"

Kimiko looked at her, then to the Queen, the King, Frigid, and finally Vael – still standing at the doorway.

"No," she said honestly. "Not now. But it's weight. It's constant. He shows me the pain they carried. The loneliness. The betrayal. And also... their beauty."

She reached up and touched the charm at her chest, which pulsed warmly under her fingers.

"He isn't trying to control me. But he's still *in me*. And I need to let him go... when the time is right."

Frigid stepped beside her sister, her expression unreadable. "Then we give you time. You've earned that and more."

The King approached, his armor catching the firelight. For the first time, his stern exterior cracked. He dropped to one knee before Kimiko and bowed his head.

"You were not my daughter," he said. "You were not born of Icelandia. But you are one of us. More than any scroll or prophecy could've predicted."

The Queen stood, her gaze filled with quiet emotion. "You've become something beyond royalty. You became the heart of this world."

Kimiko lowered her eyes, her voice soft. "I didn't come here to be a queen or a warrior. I came here to help my friends."

Freija stepped forward and rested a hand on her shoulder. "And you did, Kimi. You helped all of us. More than you know."

There was a long, quiet moment as the fire crackled.

Then the King straightened. "We'll prepare the chamber for the unbinding ritual. When you're ready, we'll begin."

Kimiko gave a small nod. "Thank you."

Outside, the snow continued to fall gently across the city of Frostholm.

But inside the chamber, the storm had finally found its center.

Bond Forged in Ice

The wind outside Freija's quarters had softened to a distant hum. For the first time in what felt like ages, peace reigned over Frostholm. The sprawling city shimmered beneath the moonlight, its rooftops bathed in soft blues and silvers. The fire in Freija's hearth crackled gently, its warmth wrapping the room in a comfort that none of the three warriors had felt in weeks.

Frigid stood near the fireplace, carefully pouring frostwine into three crystal goblets. The wine glowed faintly – a pale blue liquid drawn from the icy vineyards of the Southern slopes, rumored to be as old as the Parliament itself.

"Careful," Freija warned from her seat on the plush settee. "That stuff has kicked stronger warriors than Vael right off their feet."

Frigid arched a pale brow. "I would know. I've seen you fly into a tree after two cups."

Kimiko, nestled into the armchair closest to the fire, gave a rare laugh. It was light and unguarded, a welcome contrast to the haunted weariness she'd carried for so long. Her frostheart necklace no longer pulsed with urgency. Now, it simply glowed with a quiet, resting energy.

"You know," Freija said, accepting her glass with a wink, "the entire world nearly ended in just a few weeks. And technically, we still have two months and change left of our three-month break."

Kimiko smirked. "Any other plans for our vacation? Or is saving the planet just the warm-up act?"

Frigid brought over the remaining two glasses and handed one to each of them before taking a seat opposite them. "Perhaps we try something new. Like not nearly dying for an entire week."

They all raised their glasses.

"To peace, however long it lasts," Frigid said.

"To sisters in battle," Freija added.

"To chosen family," Kimiko finished.

The frostwine was cool and crisp, the kind of drink that lingered on the tongue with just the right blend of sweetness and strength.

Freija leaned back, arms draped over the sofa cushions. "I still can't believe you were going to let that frost elemental rip you apart without even flinching. That was insane. Noble, yes. But insane."

Kimiko shrugged, her eyes softening. "It wasn't about bravery. It was about trust. Trusting the Gatekeeper. Trusting all of you. If I didn't believe in that... I would've been gone a long time ago."

Frigid, for once, didn't respond right away. She studied her sister – her wild, impulsive, courageous sister – and then looked at Kimiko. "I used to think strength came from discipline. From standing still while the world moved. But I saw something different out there. The way you two fought together... it's something more."

Freija turned to her with a teasing grin. "Are you saying you finally approve of my off world friend?"

Frigid smiled faintly. "I'm saying... I understand now. What it means to fight side by side. To survive something bigger than yourself. That kind of bond – it's not forged by time. It's forged in fire, in frost, and in every moment when giving up would've been easier."

Kimiko met her gaze. "Then I guess we're bonded."

Freija raised her glass again. "Stronger than steel."

They clinked their glasses again and fell into quiet conversation. Stories were shared. Laughs echoed. For once, there were no missions to prepare for, no forces to defeat.

Just three women who had stood at the edge of destruction – and come back whole.

And in the heart of Freija's quarters, their friendship was sealed not by duty or destiny, but by choice.

And by love.

A Crown of Winds and Ice

A week had passed since the last elemental had been returned to its slumber.

Frostholm had not only survived – it had flourished. The skies had cleared. The storms had died. The deep groans of ice and stone had quieted, as though the very bones of the world had been soothed by the return of balance. For the first time in generations, all four continents of Icelandia were in harmony.

Within the great hall of the Frostholm fortress, banners from each continent now hung from the icy arches: silver-stitched cloths representing the East's flame, the West's stone, the South's wind, and the North's eternal frost. It was the first time such unity had been shown in this chamber since the War of Shattered Thrones.

Kimiko stood at the edge of the dais, dressed in white and silver ceremonial robes gifted to her by the Queen. Her Frostheart charm had dimmed since the ritual, no longer pulsing with the urgency of the Gatekeeper's energy, but still warm to the touch. She was flanked by Freija and Frigid, both adorned in regal formalwear rather than armor, and both beaming with quiet pride.

The chamber was packed. Leaders from every continent had arrived, each with their entourages: noble warriors from the Western cliffs, scholars robed in flame-marked silks from the East, elegant gliders and wind-dancers from the South. Vael stood near the Southern delegation, his wind-cloak draped proudly over his shoulder.

The King, dressed in full ceremonial froststeel, stepped forward. His voice echoed through the crystal-vaulted chamber.

"Today, we celebrate not just a victory," he said, "but the preservation of all that we hold dear. The heart of Icelandia beats once more in harmony. The storms have stilled. The quakes have ceased. The fires no longer rage. And the frost... has returned to sleep."

He turned to Kimiko.

"None of this would have been possible without the courage of one who did not belong to our world yet gave herself to protect it."

He paused. His gaze swept across the gathered leaders.

"Though the Gatekeeper chose her as its Vessel, it was her own heart that carried us to this moment. She endured every elemental fury, stood against powers older than time, and never faltered in her duty to balance."

Kimiko's eyes dropped briefly to the floor. She had faced death, pain, and powers beyond her comprehension – but this, standing in front of hundreds who had gathered in her honor, made her cheeks warm with a different kind of pressure.

"And she did not stand alone," the King added. He turned his gaze to Frigid and Freija. "My daughters stood beside her, as warriors and as sisters of the storm."

A soft murmur of approval rippled through the hall.

The Queen stepped forward now, her eyes bright with emotion. She held a crystal diadem in her hands – not a crown of rulership, but a circlet woven from the frozen light of the northern lights.

"In honor of your strength," she said to Kimiko, "and your heart, which proved more royal than bloodline ever could."

With solemn grace, she placed the diadem on Kimiko's head.

Then came the Icelandian ovation.

It was not clapping. Instead, each person raised a hand to their chest, palm open, and bowed deeply, a gesture reserved only for heroes. Then, one by one, they stamped their boots once upon the ground.

Boom. Boom. Boom.

A rhythmic thunder rolled through the chamber. It echoed through the pillars like a heartbeat.

Kimiko's breath caught in her throat. Not even the Gatekeeper, quiet now within her, could shield her from the overwhelming flood of emotion.

Freija leaned toward her, grinning. "Told you they liked you."

Frigid offered a rare, soft smile. "Even I must admit, you earned this."

Kimiko didn't respond right away. She was too busy trying to breathe past the lump in her throat.

But inside, something quiet – something sacred – settled.

She was home.

Even if it wasn't the world she was born in, it was one she had helped save.

And in the land of ice and balance, she had found a place where her heart could finally rest.

The Farewell of Light

The great pit beneath the palace had never felt so quiet.

The stars above were muted behind thin clouds of drifting frost, and torches along the ancient balcony burned blue with ritual fire. It was the same place where Kimiko had once stood in agony, where she had first bonded with the Gatekeeper. Now, she stood again at the edge of the platform – alone, resolute.

She had removed all ceremonial regalia, leaving only her black ninja garments beneath a simple cloak of white. Her long hair was pulled back tightly, and around her neck, the Frostheart pendant still glowed faintly, pulsing with soft light.

Frigid and Freija stood near the balcony's edge, their expressions unreadable but their eyes moist. Vael stood beside them, his arms folded, ever the silent sentinel. The King and Queen, clad in the full regalia of the High Thrones of Icelandia, flanked the ancient mages. Each mage held one of the sacred scrolls – the same that had begun the binding.

The King raised his hand.

"Gatekeeper," he called, his voice echoing against the icy walls. "We summoned you in desperation. You answered with balance. You restored our world. For that, you have our undying gratitude."

He turned his eyes to Kimiko, his voice softening. "And to you, Kimiko of Earth. Warrior of silence. Vessel of the storm. You have done what no Icelandian could. Your strength... your heart... has healed us."

Kimiko gave a small Icelandian bow.

The mages began to chant.

Their voices intertwined like a song carried on winter wind – ancient, reverent, mournful. The runes carved into the platform lit one by one, casting pale spirals of light around Kimiko's feet.

She closed her eyes.

Her breath slowed. The Gatekeeper stirred.

Soft pulses of light rose from her chest, and the Frostheart flared brightly. Her body shimmered with blue-white energy. But unlike the first ritual, there was no pain. No screaming.

Only peace.

A soft gasp escaped Kimiko's lips as the energy lifted from her. Her hands remained at her sides, open, welcoming. The light separated from her body gently, like morning mist rising from a lake.

The mist hovered before her, coalescing again into form.

A humanoid shape of swirling light and cloud, vast and tall, its form semi-solid. Eyes like stars looked down at her.

The Frostheart went dark.

Kimiko stood motionless, breathless.

Then, the Gatekeeper – now fully separate – bowed.

It was a bow not of ceremony, but of deep respect. Hands together, head low, knees bent. The ancient gesture of Earth's Eastern nations.

A tear traced down Kimiko's cheek.

The entity reached out a ghostly hand. Its index finger extended and gently tapped the Frostheart pendant. Instantly, the stone re-ignited with soft pulsing light – a heartbeat that matched her own.

Kimiko gasped softly. Her entire body seemed to fill with warmth. Not power, not energy.

Love.

The Gatekeeper bowed once more, a smaller nod this time, then turned and rose.

It spiraled upward, slowly, like a morning breeze lifting from the earth. As it reached the top of the pit, its form faded into mist, and then into nothing.

Only silence remained.

Kimiko placed both hands gently over the Frostheart.

"Thank you," she whispered, her voice thick with emotion.

She turned slowly toward the figures waiting on the balcony.

Freija's smile was radiant. Frigid had a hand over her mouth, her eyes gleaming. Vael gave a single, proud nod. The Queen reached for the King's hand.

And Kimiko's own face glowed – not with magic, but with peace.

The farewell had ended.

But the bond of hearts remained forever.

Epilogue: Light Beyond the Storm

The sun was low in the sky, its golden light diffused through wisps of soft clouds that painted the horizon in hues of lavender, rose, and amber. The glacial peaks that once loomed with threat now shimmered with gentle radiance. Melted snow pooled in calm lakes that mirrored the sky. Birds – winged and delicate – flew in lazy arcs through the air, their cries blending with the soft rustling of alpine trees that clung to the cliffs.

Freija sat at the edge of a sheer overlook, legs dangling over the drop, arms stretched behind her, supporting her as she leaned back with a satisfied sigh. Her blue skin glowed faintly in the red sunlight, and her wings were half-unfurled, catching the warm breeze.

"I told you it was beautiful," she said without turning.

Behind her, Kimiko approached more slowly, her posture still graceful but relaxed in a way that had once seemed impossible. She wore no armor now, no ceremonial robes – just a simple tunic and dark leggings that suited her agility and simplicity. The Frostheart charm still hung at her neck, its pulse gentle and steady with her heartbeat.

"It's beyond beautiful," Kimiko said softly, gazing at the endless landscape. "It feels... untouched. Pure."

Frigid was the last to arrive, gliding down from above and landing with practiced precision. She tucked her wings and stepped beside her sister, folding her arms with her usual composed expression – though today, even she had allowed a soft half-smile.

"I almost forgot this place existed," Frigid admitted. "Too many years lost to duty."

Freija patted the ground beside her. "You're making up for it now. Come on – sit down. Pretend the world isn't in crisis for once."

Frigid arched a brow but took the invitation, settling down beside her twin with surprising ease.

Kimiko moved to join them, sitting on Freija's other side. The three sat in silence for a moment, just breathing in the moment, the warmth, the peace.

Freija leaned back again. "This was the spot I wanted to show you when we first left for Icelandia, Kimiko. Remember?"

Kimiko tilted her head. "You mentioned it… right after we met back up on the Scorpion."

"Yup. This is it. My favorite view. It's the kind of place that makes you forget there's ever been war." She smirked. "Well, almost."

Kimiko gave a quiet chuckle. It was small, but genuine.

Frigid glanced between the two of them. "I used to think Freija's optimism was foolish. A distraction from the real weight of responsibility."

"You're not wrong," Freija said brightly, which earned her a nudge from Frigid.

"But," Frigid continued, "perhaps that's exactly what we need sometimes. Someone to remind us that duty doesn't always mean distance."

Kimiko looked down at her hands. "I didn't think I could ever have this. Not the power, not the respect… but the connection. The peace. It's terrifying to be vulnerable after so long."

Freija reached over and casually bumped her shoulder. "Good. That means you're human."

"Technically, I always was."

"Well, now you act like it," Freija teased.

Kimiko shook her head, a smile tugging at her lips. "You're impossible."

Frigid watched them quietly for a long moment. Then she spoke, her voice soft.

"You saved my life. And more than that – you changed it. Both of you. I may never be as loud or as carefree, but I want you to know something."

She turned to Kimiko.

"You're my sister now, too."

Kimiko blinked, completely off-guard.

Freija's eyes welled with tears. "Frigid... did you just say something emotional? Are we writing this down?"

"I swear on the Glacier Throne, Freija!"

Kimiko reached across and took Frigid's hand before the playful banter could escalate. "Thank you," she said simply, sincerely.

The three of them sat together, watching the sun dip slowly beneath the mountains. No storms lingered on the horizon. No elementals stirred. For the first time in what felt like lifetimes, peace was not an idea – but a moment.

And in that moment, laughter echoed across the cliffs – soft, strong, and shared.

Together, they watched the world bask in its light again.

About the Author

K.A. Dunlap is a storyteller with a passion for epic sci-fi adventures, fierce heroes, and high-stakes battles that shape the fate of worlds. With a background in storytelling, he has crafted a universe filled with unforgettable characters, intense action, and deep, emotional narratives that keep readers on the edge of their seats.

Inspired by the vastness of space, the resilience of warriors, and the bonds forged in battle, K.A. Dunlap weaves stories that blend cinematic action with heartfelt moments of triumph, loss, and redemption. His works explore themes of leadership, loyalty, and the enduring fight against tyranny – all set against the backdrop of a galaxy teetering on the edge of chaos.

When not writing K.A. Dunlap can be found be found exploring what this world has to offer. He enjoys good stories, especially in the sci-fi world.

The adventure is just beginning!

To learn more about the Crimson Alliance Universe go to: https://www.TheCAU.net.

Contact K.A. Dunlap @ KADunlap@TheCAU.net

Other Readings by This Author

Crimson Interlude: *Cold Front: Echoes in the Cold* is one of six interquel novels in the *Crimson Interlude* series, an extension of the *Crimson Alliance* universe first introduced in the breakout novel *A Demon's Rebellion.*

Each novel in this series explores a different set of adventures and character arcs between the epic events of the main saga, offering deeper insight into the personal journeys, battles, and bonds that shape our heroes.

Whether you're here for emotional depth, fantastical elements, sci-fi action, or character-driven storytelling, there's more waiting for you.

- **A Demon's Rebellion: The Rise of Lilith**

    Starring: The Entire Crimson Alliance team
    This is where it all begins. Follow the creation of the team and the backstory of all the characters in the Crimson Alliance Universe.
    Genre: Science Fiction, humor, drama, emotional intrigue

- **Sunlight and Shorelines: This Was Supposed to Be a Vacation**

    Starring: Adrian & Grilka
    A luxury couples-only resort. A fake honeymoon. And a sinister plot hiding beneath paradise. Adrian and Grilka's forced vacation turns into a mystery of missing guests, secret surveillance, and identity theft on a galactic scale.
    Genre: Sci-fi espionage, humor, character-driven suspense.

- **Earth and Ashes** *(Working Title)*

    Starring: Rainstorm

Returning to Earth to reconnect with her tribe, Rainstorm finds her people under siege by marauders and old enemies. But the fight for home may reveal deeper truths about her connection to the spirits and her evolving power.
Genre: Tribal sci-fi, spiritual action, emotional heritage.

- **The Scorpion Reforged** *(Working Title)*

Starring: Lilith
The Scorpion is broken, and so is Lilith—physically, emotionally, and spiritually. In a search for parts, allies, and purpose, she journeys through hostile realms and long-forgotten memories to decide what kind of leader she must become next.
Genre: Hero's journey, internal reckoning, cosmic rebuilding.

- **Crown of the Forgotten** *(Working Title)*

Starring: Nefertari
With Necra defeated, Nefertari remains behind to lead the rebuilding of Velyria and its broken systems. But while others see her as a savior, Nefertari must confront ancient local myths, political unrest, and her own doubts as she tries to restore honor to a world long ruled by fear.
Genre: Political drama, spiritual resilience, rebuilding legacy.

- **Starscarred** *(Working Title)*

Starring: Varek, Tarin & Zela
The war is over, but the stars remember. Haunted by what they've seen and changed by who they've become, Varek, Tarin, and Zela are drawn into a mission that will challenge their loyalty, test their bond, and confront the consequences of being heroes in a galaxy still healing.
Genre: Post-war mystery, squad-driven action, legacy and redemption.

www.ingramcontent.com/pod-product-compliance
Lightning Source LLC
Chambersburg PA
CBHW031953240626
47153CB00003B/963